Blues

In The Key Of

B

(Bluesday Book III)

Adrienne Thompson

Pink Cashmere Publishing Co.

Edited by Alyndria Mooney

Cover Design by Adrienne Thompson

Cover Art from dreamstime.com

Printed in the United States of America

First Printing 2013

Copyright © 2013 Adrienne Thompson

ISBN: 0988871335

ISBN-13: 978-0-9888713-3-5

Also by Adrienne Thompson:

The *Been So Long* Series:

Rapture

Been So Long

Little Sister

Been So Long 2

The *Bluesday* Series:

Bluesday

Lovely Blues

Blues In The Key Of B

Stand-alone Books:

When You've Been Blessed (Feels Like Heaven)

See Me

Thank You, Lord, for every day that you allow me to walk this earth. Thank You for the stories you give me to tell. Thank You for loving me. Thank You for teaching me to love myself.

To my readers:

I pray God's blessings over each and every one of you, and I thank you from the bottom of my heart.

RIP Bobby "Blue" Bland

RIP Trayvon Martin

Be joyful in hope, patient in affliction, faithful in prayer.

Romans 12:12 NIV

Soundtrack:

"Long Nights" *B.B. King*

"Good Morning Little School Girl" *Mississippi Fred McDowell*

"Crying Won't Help You" *B.B. King*

"Prison Bound Blues" *Bumble Bee Slim*

"Rollin' and Tumblin'" *Muddy Waters*

"Blues Is My Middle Name" *Ray Charles*

"Mean Old World Blues" *T-Bone Walker*

"Outside Help" *B.B. King*

"You Upset Me, Baby" *B.B. King*

"Information Blues" *Roy Milton*

"Sweet Little Angel" *B.B. King*

"Easy" *Walter Horton*

"My Love Is Here To Stay" *Sammy Myers*

"Highway 80 Blues" *Tommy Lee Thompson*

"How Blue Can You Get" *B.B. King*

"When The Blues Comes Knockin'" *Little Milton*

"Your Love Makes Me Feel Good" *Z.Z. Hill*

"I Done Lost My Baby" *Bumble Bee Slim*

"Down the Dirt Road Blues" *Charley Patton*

"Police Man Blues" *Sleepy John Estes*

"The Things That I Used To Do" *Guitar Slim*

"Soon As The Weather Breaks" *Bobby "Blue" Bland*

"Morning Sun Blues" *Mary Johnson*

Soundtrack (continued):

"Worried Dreamer" *Little Milton*

"Got To Find My Baby" *Little Walter*

"Things Ain't Right" *Jerry McCain*

"This I Swear" *Tyrone Davis*

"Have Mercy" *Big Walter Horton*

"Cross My Heart" *Sonny Boy Williamson*

"Feel So Bad" *Lightnin Hopkins*

"We're Ready" *Junior Wells*

"One More Shot" *Lonnie Brooks*

"Darling Baby" *Sir Charles Jones*

"Why I Sing The Blues" *B. B. King*

"Lovin' My Baby" *Big Walter Horton*

"Blues For My Baby" *Walter Trout*

"Forever" *Tyrone Davis*

"It's My Own Fault Baby" *B.B. King*

"Blues Is Here To Stay" *Bobby Warren*

"Guess Who" *B.B. King*

"Stay Around A Little Longer" *Buddy Guy Featuring B.B. King*

"Walkin' And Cryin'" *B.B. King*

"Midnight Dreams" *Big Jay McNeely*

One

"Long Nights"

Bobbie

Faith's shrill cries awakened me from a shallow sleep. I quickly stumbled to my feet and, with closed eyes, shuffled across the room to her crib. She had her own room, but it was just easier to let her sleep in our bedroom. After three months of midnight diaper changes and feedings, I should've been used to this, but I wasn't. As a singer, I'd lost count of how many all-nighters I'd pulled with concerts and after-parties, and after-after-parties. But this was different. There was no music and this was not fun for me. I was so tired and my wonderful, handsome, loving husband was proving to be little to no help.

I gently lifted my little girl into my arms, sat in the rocking chair next to her crib, and began to breast-feed her. I looked down at her and sighed. She was a beautiful little combination of me and Reggie with soft, brown skin and curly, black hair. I leaned my head back against the chair and closed my eyes. I hated feeling this way, resenting having to care for my own child—a child Reggie and I fervently prayed for. But despite my best efforts to shake my feelings, I couldn't.

I opened my eyes and looked over at Reggie, who hadn't so much as moved a muscle. It was unfair. It really was. I had no choice but to get up every time the baby woke up. I was breast-feeding her. I *had* to get up. And though breast-feeding had been a mutual decision, I couldn't help but feel like I'd gotten the short end of the stick.

Tears began to fill my eyes. *What is wrong with me? Why do I feel this way?* I wondered as I blinked back tears and took a deep breath. Three months had passed and I still felt the same way I'd felt when we first brought Faith home—detached. I felt like I was holding someone else's baby. I didn't feel like her mother. I didn't feel like *anyone's* mother for that matter. There was no connection. No bond. Sure, I fed her and changed her and bathed her, but those things felt more like chores than motherhood. When was my motherly instinct going to kick in? When was I going to start to love my baby?

I gently pulled her from my breast, and held her against my chest to burp her. I breathed in her fresh scent and looked down at her little body and wished I knew what was wrong with me. *Maybe I'm crazy. Maybe I need to see a shrink.* I quickly dismissed those thoughts. How could I explain to Reggie and then a doctor that I didn't love my own child? They'd surely have me committed. No, this was something I'd have to figure out how to deal with on my own. I'd just have to *make* myself love her.

She burped softly and then rested her little head against my shoulder. I closed my eyes and rocked a few more minutes before placing her back into her crib then returning to bed. As I settled in under the covers, Reggie draped his arm across my waist and snuggled close to me.

"Everything okay?" he asked.

I stared across the room, through the darkness, at the crib. "Everything's fine," I lied.

***

"Are you sure you're okay, Mama?" I asked as I clutched the phone with one hand and tried to change Faith's diaper with the other.

"I'm fine, Bobbie Ann. You gon' hafta stop all dis worrin'. You 'bout ta drive me crazy! I feel jus' fine," Mama replied.

"Well, you sound tired."

"I *am* tired. I'm a old woman raisin' two teenagers. I gotta right ta be tired."

"Well, how are the girls?"

After a moment of hesitation she said, "They fine."

I sighed. "Mama, what's wrong? Is it Tomeka again?"

Since my brother had been arrested for trying to rob a pawn shop and then was subsequently charged with her mother's murder, Tomeka had been more than a handful—skipping school, talking back, refusing to do her chores. I was sure Mama was tired of dealing with her.

"Naw, she okay."

"Mama…"

Mama sighed heavily into the phone. "I got her report card yesterday. She flunkin' jus' 'bout all of her classes. She a smart girl. I jus' don't know what's goin' on wit' her."

I finished snapping Faith's onesie and picked her up. I carried her through the house and sat down on the sofa with her. "Well, maybe Junior can talk some sense into her. I still plan to take her and Sharee to see him on Saturday."

"Yeah, well, I hope so. Seem like whenever she see him she get worse, though. I did my best by her and Sharee but maybe it's jus' them bad genes passed down from Junior's real daddy. I don't know."

I was shocked to hear my mama say something as faithless as that. In my mind, she'd always been a pillar of faith. It was her strong faith that had brought her to the other side of a fatal cancer diagnosis. "You don't sound like yourself, Mama. You sure you're okay?"

"Whachu mean I don't sound like myself?"

"I mean you're acting like this situation is hopeless. I've never heard you sound like that before. I've always heard you speak faith to situations like this."

There was silence from Mama.

"Mama, you still there?"

"Yeah, I'm here. Don't feel good when yo' own child make more sense than you do, but you right. I'ma pray and ask da' Lord how ta handle dis. And speakin' of faith, how is my grandbaby?"

It was my turn to be silent. I looked down at Faith who peered up at me innocently.

"Bobbie Ann, you still there?" Mama asked.

"Uh, yes, ma'am."

"Did you hear me? I asked about da baby."

"Oh, you were breaking up. I couldn't hear you. She's fine. She's in my lap right now."

"Humph, you don't sound right, yourself. Sound different."

I sighed, again. "Just tired. I'm still trying to get used to her schedule. Trying to get adjusted."

Mama laughed softly. "Well, I can tell you right now, you ain't never gon' get adjusted, 'cause as soon as you thank you got a handle on thangs, they gon' change."

"Yeah," I said absently.

"Bobbie Ann, you sho' everythang okay?"

"Oh, yes, ma'am. Like I said, I'm just tired."

"You need me ta come out there? I can come help you if you need me to,"

"No, ma'am. I can't ask you to do that. You've got the girls. We're fine, really."

"Okay, well, let me git off dis phone and cook some dinner. Bye, Bobbie Ann."

"Bye, Mama." I hung the phone up, looked down at my daughter, and cried.

Two

"Good Morning Little School Girl"

Tomeka

Dear Tomeka,

Thanks for letting me write to you. I'm glad you are willing to get to know me better. It gets lonely in here without someone to talk to and share your thoughts with. I've made a lot of mistakes, I can't deny that. I can't deny that I used to be a bad person, but drugs will do that to you. The drugs kept me from thinking straight. If I had been thinking straight, I never would've done those bad things. But I can't blame the drugs, either, because I'm the one who decided to use them. No one made me do it.

It was fun at first, but it got out of control and before I knew it, I was hooked and willing to do anything to get more drugs. I hurt the people who cared the most about me. I hurt everyone around me, and I'm sorry for that. I'm working hard to change and to be a better man. Well, I just wanted to let you know that I've been thinking about you, and I hope to see you soon. Write back, okay?

Love,

Abraham

I finished reading the letter and then read it over again. I read it ten times before folding it back up and sliding it under my mattress. I smiled as I rolled over in bed and pulled the covers over my head. Sharee was fast asleep as I closed my eyes and tried to picture Abraham's face. I'd met him during one of my visits to my dad in prison. He was a little taller than me and he was so handsome with these big brown eyes. His wore his hair spiked and when I first saw him, it felt like my heart actually stopped. I was on my way to the restroom when I passed by his table. He was visiting with his mother and sister.

As I walked past his table, our eyes locked, and I got this funny feeling—like we were connected or something. When I left the bathroom, I ran right into his sister. She handed me a note from him. On it he told me I was pretty. We'd been passing notes between his sister ever since. Well, actually we'd both been mailing our letters to her, and she'd been forwarding them to me and Abraham. Since I was only sixteen and Abraham was twenty-two, we had to keep our relationship a secret, but I didn't mind. It kind of made things even more exciting.

I smiled at the thought of him, of his face and his smile. I was so excited about visiting my dad that weekend because it meant I would get to see Abraham Rios, even if it was from afar.

***

Dear Abraham,

I am so glad you wrote to me. Don't worry. I don't hold your past against you. I know what drugs can do to a person. My dad was into them real bad, but I guess you know that. So was my mom. My dad killed my mom over drugs, did you know that? Yeah, I know. Messed up, huh? It really bothered me for a while. But I don't care anymore. I mean, she was never around anyway. Neither was my dad until last year. Then he ran out on me and my sister again. At first, I was hurt about that, too. But I don't care about that anymore, either.

I used to be really sad a lot. I used to cry all the time and I used to want to die so bad. But since I met you and you've been writing me, I feel so much better. I don't feel as sad anymore. I—

"Tomeka Brooks, do you know the answer to number three?" Mrs. Stark asked.

I slammed my hand on top of the paper and looked up at the dry erase board. I hadn't been paying attention to what was going on in class. I frowned a little, and for about a second, actually tried to work the problem out in my head. Then I decided I'd better just give her some kind of answer before she came to my desk and saw what I'd really been doing. So, I said, "Three?"

Mrs. Stark raised her eyebrows and nodded. "Correct."

I let out the breath I'd been holding and gave her a little smile. I had no idea how I managed to guess the correct answer. But I was glad I did. Out of the hot seat, I turned my attention back to my letter:

I can't wait to see you when I come visit my dad. Tell your sister I said "thank you" for giving you my letters. See you soon.

Love,

Tomeka

Three

"Crying Won't Help You"

Bobbie

I pasted on my best smile as I walked into the church behind Reggie. Reggie was smiling, laughing, shaking hands, and proudly lifting the baby carrier, showing Faith to anyone with eyes to see. He was a genuinely proud papa and every member of the congregation could easily see it. I nodded and smiled and shook hands, all the while wishing we could've snuck in through one of the side doors and taken our seats without all of the hoopla. But that was a wasted wish since Reggie was the assistant pastor.

We finally made it to the front pew, and Reggie sat the carrier on the pew beside me and then leaned over and kissed Faith on the forehead. Then he took my hand and kissed it before leaving for his seat in the pulpit. I stared after him, wishing he could stay with us, because I just didn't want to be alone with her. Being alone with her meant that if she woke up during service I'd have to take her out of the sanctuary, into the bathroom, and change and feed her, and I just didn't feel like doing any of that. I turned my head and looked down at my sleeping baby and felt my eyes begin to fill with tears. I felt so bad about feeling like she was a burden, but that's exactly how I felt. I felt like I'd been saddled with this huge responsibility that I just wasn't ready for. Maybe that's why we'd had so much trouble getting pregnant at first. Maybe I just wasn't meant to be a mother.

I sighed and turned my attention to the choir stand as the music began to play. I half-heartedly sang along with the choir and spent most of the service praying that Faith wouldn't wake up, but of course she did.

About halfway through the sermon she began to squirm and whimper. I closed my eyes for a second, and when I opened them Reggie was staring at me with raised eyebrows. One look around the sanctuary told me that Faith was disturbing service. All eyes were on me as I stood and carried her out of the church. In the ladies' restroom, I closed us off in the largest stall, sat on the toilet, and breast fed her with a river of tears flowing from my eyes.

After I finished feeding her, I laid her across my lap and changed her diaper. Then I just sat there in my nice, powder blue dress and matching hat and stared at the stall walls. I just couldn't bear the thought of walking back into that sanctuary and feeling all of those curious eyes on me. So I sat there until I heard a steady stream of women entering and leaving the small restroom—signaling that service was over. I cautiously left the restroom and made my way back to my seat in the sanctuary where I waited for Reggie to finish fellowshipping with the other preachers and worshippers.

I tried to look busy, gathering the diaper bag and my purse and securing Faith in the carrier—hoping that no one would come over and try to talk to me. Of course it didn't work. When I looked up for a second, Sister Purifoy was headed in my direction. She was tall and wide and as sweet as a peach cobbler, but I wasn't in the mood to talk to anyone, including her.

But nevertheless, I smiled and said, "Hello, Sister Purifoy."

She rested her hand on my shoulder and offered me a sincere smile. "Hello there, sweetheart. Is everything okay with the little bundle of joy? You were back there with her for nearly the whole sermon."

As sweet as Sister Purifoy was, I had to bite my tongue to keep from telling her that I knew exactly where I'd been and that I didn't need her to remind me. "Yes, ma'am. She's fine now. She was just a little fussy," I lied in a syrupy sweet tone.

Sister Purifoy smiled. "Well, I know how that can be. Raised five boys all by myself after my husband left. And not one of them was the same. Why, Charlie, my oldest, was an angel. He barely cried at all. Now Lynus, the second oldest, he cried bloody murder every night. He was so colicky it nearly drove me crazy…"

She continued her little trip down baby memory lane and I smiled and nodded and "oh'd" and "ah'd" while silently wishing Reggie would come and rescue me. Finally she ended with, "Well, if you ever need anyone to babysit, I'd love to. I just love babies. No charge, of course."

"Well, thank you, sister. I just might take you up on that offer," I replied.

Her eyes lit up. "I sure hope so." She peered at Faith in her carrier. "I'd love to spend some time with this precious little angel. She's a beautiful little thing."

"Thank you." I looked up to see Reggie finally coming our way. I stood from the pew and picked up the carrier. "Well, I'll see you next week, sister."

"Alright, honey." She turned her attention to Reggie. "Y'all take care of that little angel, Rev. Darrough."

Reggie smiled as he took the baby from me. "You know we will, sister."

I followed Reggie out of the church and into our vehicle. We were on our way home when he said, "What happened today?"

I started to pretend that I didn't hear him, but I dismissed that idea. "What do you mean?" I asked with my eyes fixed on the windshield.

"During service. Faith started crying and it looked like you'd zoned out or something, like you didn't hear her."

I dropped my eyes to my lap. "I don't know. I think I'm just tired or something. Things haven't been easy for me, you know?"

He reached over and rested his hand on my knee. "What's wrong, baby?"

I wanted to tell him the truth, but I just didn't know how to. How do you tell your husband that you don't like taking care of your own child— *his* child? I closed my eyes and sighed. "I don't know. Just hormones, I guess. I'm just tired."

Reggie patted my knee and said, "I tell you what, when we get home, I'll take care of Faith. You take a nap and rest yourself, okay?"

I looked over at him and nodded. "Okay."

Four

"Prison Bound Blues"

Tomeka

Aunt Bobbie Ann picked us up Friday afternoon and took us to her and Uncle Reggie's house in Houston. We spent the night with them. I always loved spending the night with them. Sharee and I had so much fun playing with the baby, and Aunt Bobbie Ann didn't fuss all the time like Granny. All that fussing was getting old with me. I mean, after all, I was almost grown. I had a mind of my own, and I was tired of having to obey her every word. What did she know about life, anyway? She had never lived anywhere but Willisville, which was *nowhere*. Nothing but the sticks, if you ask me. Who would want to spend their whole life there? Not me. After my eighteenth birthday, I was going to leave that place for good, just like my parents did. The only difference was that I wasn't going to get strung out on no drugs like them. I was going to be a model or maybe a singer like Aunt Bobbie Ann. I could carry a tune and with enough practice, maybe I could be as good as her.

I looked over at my little sister. I loved her. I really did, and I hated that I was going to have to leave her behind, but I had to do what I had to do. She actually *liked* living with Granny. I had no idea why, but she did. I mean, Granny wouldn't even let us have a computer or internet, talking

13

about "Da intranet ain't nuthin' but da devil." *What-ever.*

And Sharee actually liked visiting our daddy at the prison, too. Now, that was just crazy. I faked like I liked it, but I really didn't care about seeing him. I was just in it for the trip away from home and the chance to see Abraham.

I turned and looked out the window of Uncle Reggie's truck and smiled. I always smiled when I thought about Abraham. Thinking about him made me happy. Maybe if I didn't make it as a model or a singer, me and Abraham could get married. He could get a job, and I could stay home with the kids. We could have two—a boy and a girl. What would we name them? The boy would be Abraham, Jr. for sure. But the girl? I'd have to think about that.

"What you girls back there daydreaming about?" Uncle Reggie asked.

I smiled into the rearview mirror.

"I'm thinking about little Faith," Sharee said. "I can't wait to get back to y'all's house so I can play with her some more."

Uncle Reggie smiled. "I miss her, too. What about you, Meka? What's on your mind?"

"Uh, same thing," I said.

"What about you, baby," he said softly as he placed his hand on Aunt Bobbie's knee.

Aunt Bobbie Ann smiled. "Um…same thing."

"You worried about her?" he asked.

Aunt Bobbie Ann shrugged.

"It's okay. I think she's in good hands with Sis. Purifoy. She's got experience with babies, and you left plenty of breast milk. It'll only be for a few hours," Uncle Reggie said.

Aunt Bobbie Ann nodded.

I sighed. I hoped that one day Abraham and me would be just like Aunt Bobbie Ann and Uncle Reggie. They met in high school and now they were so happy and they had a beautiful baby. I closed my eyes and tried to picture myself in a wedding dress walking down the aisle towards Abraham. I pictured the smile he'd have on his face. When I drifted off to sleep in the backseat, I was picturing our daughter, a little brown princess just like Faith. Maybe we could name her after Abraham's sister—Claudia.

***

I was so nervous when we walked into the prison. My hands were shaking when I took my shoes off and walked through the metal detector thing. I could barely get them tied after I put them back on. Sharee was smiling the whole time. You would've thought we were going to the mall or something.

We walked into a room that was full of tables and sat at one near the windows in the back. I didn't understand why they had windows in there, because all you could see through them was prison and more prison, and you could barely see that with that metal stuff covering them. Not bars but more like a fence or something.

We sat there and waited for Daddy to come out and Aunt Bobbie Ann looked like she hated being there even more than I did. Uncle Reggie held her hand and whispered something in her ear and she smiled. I smiled, too, but not because of them. I smiled because a couple of tables over I saw Abraham's sister and mother. I knew it wouldn't be long before I'd get to see Abraham. The only problem was that there was a better view of his table from Sharee's seat.

"Switch seats with me," I whispered to her.

"Why?" she asked.

"Because I wanna sit there."

"Why?"

"I just do."

"What difference does it make?"

"Come on, Sharee, just switch with me. *Please?*"

She sighed loudly as she gave up her seat. I quickly hopped up and we switched.

"Y'all playing musical chairs?" Uncle Reggie asked.

"No, I just like this seat better," I replied.

"Well, y'all better get settled. Here comes your daddy," he said.

I looked up to see my daddy headed in our direction, and walking in right behind him was Abraham. My heart started to beat so fast I was scared it was going to explode or stop or something. I guess that's what love feels like—exciting and scary. At least that's how *I* felt.

Daddy made it to the table and hugged Sharee and then Aunt Bobbie Ann. He shook Uncle Reggie's hand and then he turned to me. Things were always very awkward between me and my daddy because, of the two of us—me and Sharee—I was the one who had wanted things to work out the worst. When he showed back up in our lives a little over a year earlier, I was so excited. I loved being with him and his fiancée at the time. I liked listening to him have a good time with his friends. Sharee hated it all. She was glad when he disappeared on us. I never forgave him for it, and I didn't know if I ever would.

"Can I have a hug, Meka?" he asked cautiously.

I nodded and gave him a stiff hug. Then we all sat down and Daddy started with the same old questions he asked us every visit: "How's school? How are your grades? You feeling okay? Y'all obeying your Granny?" Then he'd start asking about Granny, as if he really cared: "How's Mama? Things okay at the house? Her cancer still in remission?" And then he'd start on Aunt Bobbie Ann and Uncle Reggie: "How're y'all doing? How's the baby? You back in the studio yet, sis? You 'bout ready to hit the road, ain't you? You heard from Dee?" Dee was once his fiancée until he messed that up. I just sat there and listened to his bull crap and wished he'd just shut up.

And while my father faked caring about someone other than himself, I turned my attention to Abraham. He was talking to his mother, but his eyes were focused on me. When I looked in his direction, he smiled at me. I smiled back at him, and then I covered my mouth with my hand because I was so happy I almost started giggling. If I did that, everyone at my table would think I was crazy. But of course, Bloodhound-Sharee noticed anyway.

"What you laughing about?" she asked.

"Nothing. I ain't laughing." Then I shot her a look that said, "You better shut up *or else*."

Sharee rolled her eyes. "Whatever."

"I need to use the restroom," I said to no one in particular.

"Okay, you want me to go with you?" Aunt Bobbie Ann asked.

"No, I'll be alright."

As I stood to leave the table, Daddy grabbed my wrist. "Be careful. It's some crazy people in here," he whispered.

I wanted to say, "You mean like you?" But I just widened my eyes like I was really scared and nodded. Then I left our table and slowly walked through the room, slowing even more when I passed Abraham's table.

"Ahí está mi bebé," Abraham said loudly.

I didn't know what he said, but he was looking right at me when he said it and his voice made me tingle all over. I was grinning from ear to ear by the time I made it into the restroom.

I shut myself inside a stall and closed my eyes and imagined what it would be like to kiss him and to hug him, and then, when the time was right, what it would feel like to *be* with him.

"Tomeka, you in here?" a voice asked. I opened the stall door and was face-to-face with Abraham's sister, Claudia. "Oh, good. I have a message from Abraham," she said.

I nodded. "Okay."

She grabbed both of my hands. "He says his heart is full with love for you. He thanks God for you every day and he cannot wait for the two of you to be together. And he wanted me to give you this." She handed me a neatly folded piece of paper.

I took it and smiled. Then I pulled a letter from the back pocket of my jeans. "This is for him. Tell him I love him, too."

She nodded, and with a smile, left the bathroom. I went back into the stall and opened his letter.

Dear Tomeka,

As I write this letter, I am laying on my bunk. It is the middle of the night and everything is still and quiet. Things are hardly ever quiet in here. But when they are it makes me feel free. It makes me feel like I'm back home in my own bed. You know what else makes me feel like that? You do. Every time I get a letter from you or see you at visitation, I feel free and I feel hope. That's what you are to me, Tomeka. You are my hope for better things. You are my hope for a better life.

I love you and I thank God for you. Cielito. Mi amor.

Love,

Abraham

I was reading the letter for the third time when I heard Aunt Bobbie Ann's voice. "Tomeka, is that you in there? You okay?"

I quickly folded up the letter and shoved it into my pocket as I flushed the toilet. "Yes, ma'am. Here I come." I left the stall and walked to the sink.

"Is it your stomach?" she asked.

I nodded. "I think I ate too much ice cream last night."

After I washed and dried my hands, she smiled and wrapped her arm around my shoulder. "Well, no ice cream tonight. Come on, we're getting ready to leave in a little bit."

I nodded. "Okay."

As we passed by Abraham's table on our way back to our own table, my eyes met his and my heart started to race again. I loved him so much, but the best thing was that he loved me, too.

Five

"Rollin' and Tumblin'"

Bobbie

As I climbed into Reggie's truck and fastened the seatbelt, I breathed a sigh of relief. The visits to my brother were always tense. It was plain to see that Tomeka hadn't forgiven him and that she still harbored hard feelings towards him. She spent most of the visit in the restroom and when she was at the table, she could barely stand to look at him. As a matter of fact, she kept her eyes across the room most of the time. She'd even switched seats with her sister so that she wouldn't have to sit next to him.

Junior had disappointed all of us time and time again, and that disappointment was never easy to deal with. But I knew my disappointment was nothing in comparison to Sharee and Tomeka's pain. He was their father, and besides the fact that he spent most of their lives addicted to drugs and roaming from place to place, he also murdered their mother.

Now he claimed he was really clean and wanted to start over with them, with all of us, but I couldn't help wondering if his words were sincere or if being behind bars was the reason for his repentant attitude. I knew the same thoughts were running through the girls' minds as well. But like me, they had been willing to give him at least a little bit of the benefit of the doubt. After all, just because he'd failed to truly clean up his act in the past didn't mean he'd fail this time. All any of us could do was hope for the best.

I peered out the windshield at the highway in front of us and sighed. For the first time that day, I wondered how Faith was doing. I hoped she and Sis. Purifoy were getting along okay. If this babysitting thing worked out, maybe Sis. Purifoy would be willing to keep her more often. Maybe I'd even get to start preparing for my tour a little earlier than planned. That would be great.

I glanced over at Reggie and reality kicked back in. We'd already discussed my going back to work. Six months—that's what we'd decided. It would be best to wait until Faith was six months-old. It would be best for her. But what about what would be best for me? Would it be best for me to spend six whole months cooped up in the house with a baby? Reggie had already gone back to work. How was that fair? Why was the mother expected to sacrifice her life for the child and not the father?

I closed my eyes and tried to steady my breathing because the thoughts in my head were making me angrier and angrier. It just wasn't right that I had to put my life on hold and Reggie didn't. Then, another thought entered my mind: *Shouldn't I want to be with my baby all the time? Isn't that what's normal?* I rested my elbow on the arm rest and clutched my forehead. Was I going crazy? Why did I feel this way? What was wrong with me?

"Hey, you okay over there?" Reggie asked.

I looked over at him to see him staring back at me with concern in his eyes. How could I be mad at this man when he was so good to me? "I'm okay. Just tired," I replied.

He smiled the smile that made me fall in love with him so many years ago. "Well, sit back and relax, baby. Take a nap if you want to. We'll be home in a couple of hours."

I returned his smile. "I love you."

He reached over and gently rubbed my cheek with his thumb. "I love you more."

***

It was after dark when we returned home. The girls were out of the car racing towards the house before Reggie could open my door. He took my hand and kissed me once I was standing on the driveway. Then he led me into the house. I half-expected to be greeted by Faith's inconsolable cries, but the house was quiet. While the girls headed to the bathroom, I headed upstairs to Faith's room where Sis. Purifoy was sitting in the rocking chair with Faith in her arms. She was humming an old hymn and Faith was fast asleep. I stood in the doorway and smiled.

Sensing my presence, Sis. Purifoy looked up at me and smiled. "Y'all back so soon? Me and the little one was just getting to know each other."

I slowly moved towards them. "I hope she wasn't too much trouble. I really appreciate you for keeping her."

Sis. Purifoy frowned. "Trouble? Why, it was my pleasure to keep this little angel! Being around children keeps you young. Anytime you need me, I'm available. Shoot, I ain't doing nothing else but piddling around my house. Makes me feel good to do something useful."

She handed me the baby. "Well, thank you, again, Sis. Purifoy. I just may call on you to keep her in a couple of weeks."

Sis. Purifoy bent over and kissed Faith's forehead. "Anytime, sweetie. Anytime."

Reggie arrived just in time to walk Sis. Purifoy to her car. I gently laid Faith in her crib and as I moved to turn off the light, she began to cry and my heart began to race. For a moment, I didn't know how to react or what to do. My chest felt tight and I could barely breathe. I closed my eyes and leaned against the wall as the baby continued to cry. I slid to the floor and tried to steady my breathing, but I couldn't.

Sharee and Tomeka appeared in the doorway with concerned looks on their faces, and all I could do was to clutch my chest and try not to pass out. But it was no use. Seconds later, darkness surrounded me.

Six

"Blues Is My Middle Name"

Bobbie

I had a panic attack—a period of intense fear or apprehension. Or at least that's what the emergency room doctor said after he checked me out and I explained to him what happened. I guess I couldn't argue with that, because I was very apprehensive about taking care of my child, but how in the world could I explain that to him or to my husband? I was out of my mind for feeling that way and I knew it.

"Your baby, how old is he?" the doctor asked.

"*She's* three months-old," I answered.

"I see. Mrs. Darrough, do you have a history of depression or anxiety?"

I stared down at my hands which were clenched tightly in my lap. "I…I almost drank myself to death once. Does that count as depression?"

With raised eyebrows he said, "Yes, definitely."

I looked up at him. "You think I'm depressed now?"

"Well, I know that women with a history of depression are at risk for developing postpartum depression. Have you felt hopeless or tearful since giving birth?"

I nodded.

"Have you found it hard to take care of your daughter because of these feelings?"

I nodded again as tears began to fill my eyes. "Yes."

"Mrs. Darrough, do you feel ashamed because of how you feel?"

The tears flooded my cheeks. "Yes, I do."

He wrote something on a pad and then handed two sheets of paper to me. "I've written you a prescription for an antidepressant, and on the other slip of paper is the name and number of a very good psychiatrist who specializes in treating postpartum depression."

I took the papers from him and wiped my cheeks. "Thank you. Can you send my husband in now, please?"

He gave me an encouraging smile as he left.

Minutes later, Reggie entered the small room, his face full of worry as he walked over to me and cupped my face in his hands. "Is everything alright? What did the doctor say?"

I looked up at him. "He told me what I already knew but couldn't face."

The concern in his eyes deepened. "What, baby? What is it?"

"I've been struggling with some feelings and I should have told you sooner, but I was afraid of what you've think of me if you knew."

"Knew what, Bobbie Ann? Don't you know there's nothing you can say to make me think badly of you? I love you."

I nodded as new tears began to fall. "I know. I was...I was just ashamed of feeling this way."

"What way? Please tell me what's wrong."

I sighed woefully. "Ever since we brought Faith home, I've just felt really disconnected from her. She makes me feel trapped. I...I...don't like taking care of her." And then the floodgates opened, and I cried enough tears to drown in.

Reggie was silent, confusion and shock clouding his face. He didn't know what to say. He hadn't been expecting to hear what I'd just told him.

"The-the-the doctor says it's postpartum depression. He-he gave me a prescription and he suggested I see a psychiatrist. He said it's common for women with a history of depression to suffer from this."

Still nothing from Reggie.

I dropped my head and sobbed. "I'm sorry, Reggie. I want to love her. I really do. I'm sorry I'm so messed up. You deserve better. I told you that a long time ago. I'm so sorry."

Reggie placed his hands on my arms and brought his face close to mine. "Stop that. You are everything to me. There's no one better for me than you. You can't help how you feel, Bobbie. It's not your fault. You love Faith. Whether you know it or not, *I* know it. We'll get through this. This is not the end of the world. We will get through it." He lifted my chin until we were eye-to-eye. "Do you hear me, Bobbie Ann? We will get through this—me and you. I love you." Then he pulled me into his arms and for the first time since Faith's birth, I felt like everything would really be alright.

***

I don't think a woman ever loved a man as much as I loved Reggie Wayne Darrough. He was, hands down, the kindest, gentlest, most understanding man in the world. After I was discharged from the hospital, Reggie took me home, and after a long discussion, we both decided to increase the baby's bottle feedings so that he could help me more with her. We also decided to have Sis. Purifoy keep her a couple of days a week— one night so that we could be alone together, and one day so that I could have time to think and breathe without having to worry about the baby.

The changes helped tremendously. I no longer felt like someone was holding a pillow of motherhood over my face, pressing down and cutting off my air supply. I could breathe again. I could think clearly, and stepping back from the situation a little made me realize that Reggie was right. I did love my daughter. I was just overwhelmed from the enormous responsibility that went along with being a new mother. I was glad I'd finally confided in Reggie. I was glad he stood by my side and didn't think any less of me for feeling the way I felt. I was glad to be his wife.

Seven

"Mean Old World Blues"

Tomeka

I needed to figure out a way to convince Granny to get me a cell phone. In his last letter, Abraham said that his sister had snuck a burner phone in to him and that if I had a phone, he could call me. I needed a phone, and I needed one *bad*. In all the months we'd been writing back and forth, I'd gotten to know Abraham really well. I loved him a lot, but I hardly ever heard his voice and I really wanted to.

I sat in my room staring at the wall, glad to be alone. I'd played sick so that I could miss church. I was pretty sure Granny didn't believe me. Maybe she just didn't feel like fussing, but that was a scary thought because the last time she didn't feel like fussing, she had cancer. I sure hoped her cancer wasn't back. Yeah, I got tired of her sometimes, but I didn't want her to die.

There had to be a way to convince her to buy me a phone. Or maybe if I asked Aunt Bobbie Ann, she would get me one. The only thing was that she'd have to run it by Granny, first. I sighed. I was almost grown and I'd already had a phone once, but when my daddy disappeared and his girlfriend, Dee, dropped me and Sharee off like dirty laundry, it got cut off. I still had the phone, it just didn't work. I had asked granny if she would get it cut back on, and all she had to say was that I didn't need it. How could she tell me what I needed? Like I said, I was almost grown!

I had some money I'd saved up from the allowance Aunt Bobbie Ann gave me and Sharee every month. I could pay for a phone or at least buy some minutes myself, but my only ride to the store was with Granny. Maybe I could get Aunt Bobbie Ann to take me to the store the next time she took us to Houston, and I could sneak and buy some minutes or something. But that was weeks away, and I needed a phone ASAP.

I groaned as I climbed out of bed and walked over to my little desk. I grabbed a piece of paper and began to write.

Dear Abraham,

I was so glad to get your letter the other day. I always love reading your letters. You make me feel so happy. I'm sorry I won't get to see you this month, but my aunt that usually brings me to visitation got sick after my last visit, and she said she needs some time to rest. But she promised to bring me and my sister to see our father next month. But bump that, you know I'm only coming to see you.

I'm trying to figure out how to get a phone so you can call me. Do you think your sister would send me one like yours if I send her the money? I know she's already doing a lot for me and you, and I hate to even ask for another favor. But it's the only thing I could come up with. Anyway, I'm home alone right now. My granny and my sister are gone to church which, if you ask me, is a waste of time. All that shouting and praying is just dumb, and I didn't feel like it today.

Well, I hope you're doing okay in there. I miss you, Abraham.

Love,

Tomeka

I folded the letter up and put in an envelope. I'd stick it in the mailbox on the way to the bus stop the next morning.

***

Dear Tomeka,

I was glad to get your letter. It is always a blessing to hear from you. Yes, I'm fine. I hate being in here, but I try to make the most of it. Your dad seems like a pretty cool guy. We both go to chapel together. He can sing, too. Did you know that? He sang a gospel song the other night that almost made me cry. And I don't cry easily. Anyway, I kind of wish he knew about us, but I know I can't tell him because of your age. Plus, no father would want his daughter to be with a former drug-addicted, dope-selling convict. And that's what I am, mi amor. I'm a good-for-nothing convict and you deserve better.

So that's why I've decided to leave you alone. I love you, Tomeka. I really do. But this is wrong. You're too young, and I can't ask you to wait around for me or sneak behind your grandmother's back to write and talk to me anymore. I'm sorry I ever started this. You should go on with your life and forget about me.

And don't feel that way about church. Praying is good, Tomeka. God loves us. He loves you. Don't forget that.

Love,

Abraham

I held the paper to my chest and sat down next to the mailbox. I didn't understand. How could he break up with me like that? He said he loved me. Now he was gone, just like every other man who ever said he loved me. My grandpa loved me and he died. My father loved me and he left me over and over again. Now Abraham was gone. What was wrong so with me that no one loved me enough to stay? I sat there and cried as I watched the sun go down, and then I walked back to the house.

Eight

"Outside Help"

Bobbie

The blues comes and the blues goes

Why it won't leave me alone, Lord only knows

I'm a good woman, nothing but love in my heart

Just wanna move on from the blues and make a brand new start...

The words to that old song of mine couldn't have been truer as I sat across from Dr. Angela Bradford and sighed. *Been there, done that, got several t-shirts,* I thought—my mind reverting to my past, my alcoholism, and subsequent therapy. For some reason, after all I'd been through, I thought I was fixed. It had been years since I'd taken a drink or felt depressed. Years, that is, until I brought Faith home. With her arrival came a flood of feelings and issues I really thought were long gone. Guess I thought wrong.

Dr. Bradford offered me a nice smile and began her spiel—who she was, where she was from, what she was going to help me do. She was nice enough, but I was honestly feeling better. I felt like the steps me and Reggie had taken to ease the load on me were really helping. I was much less overwhelmed, and I was beginning to feel like Faith was less of a burden. I was actually beginning to connect with her.

So why did I still need to sit in that chair and spill my guts to a stranger when I really didn't want to? I sighed and tried to smile when she asked me to tell her about myself.

"My name is Bobbie Darrough. I'm married to a wonderful man. We have one child, a daughter named Faith. I'm a singer by profession. Um, I'm a recovering alcoholic and I try to attend AA meetings as often as I can, but that's been difficult with the new baby and all. I'm here because of some depression and anxiety I've been dealing with since the birth of my daughter." I said this hoping to answer all of the questions I knew she probably had written on the legal pad that was sitting on the desk in front of her.

She nodded and gave me a knowing look. "Okay. Bobbie, do you have a goal for the work we will do here?"

"A goal? Well, yeah. I want to stop having chest pains and passing out every time my baby cries," I said sarcastically. "Don't you have my chart? Don't you know what's going on with me? I have postpartum depression."

"So your goal is to be able to take care of your baby without anxiety?"

Duh. "Yes. That would be about it."

"Mrs. Darrough, I sense some animosity. Are you here of your own volition?"

I suddenly felt a little ashamed of my own behavior. It wasn't this woman's fault that I was so messed up. But whose fault was it? Mine? At any rate, I needed to get to the bottom of this thing. I needed to know *why* I was having this anxiety.

"I'm sorry. Yes, I'm here because I want to be here. It's just that, I feel like I'm running in circles. I underwent therapy back when I first realized I was an alcoholic and I really thought I had my life together, and now this. It's all just very frustrating. I just wish I could be normal."

She smiled. "Well, normal is a relative word, Mrs. Darrough."

"You can call me Bobbie if you want."

"Okay, Bobbie. There's nothing abnormal about being apprehensive about a major change in your life. I'm going to help you work through things, get to the bottom of some issues, and give you some coping techniques. Does that sound like it would be beneficial to you?"

I nodded. "Yes, and thank you."

"Alright, first tell me about your marriage. How were things before the baby was born?"

I crossed my legs and sighed as I thought for a moment. My eyes traveled around the warmly decorated room. "Well, we've had our ups and downs like most couples, but we've always managed to work things out. We are totally committed to each other and Reggie is the most forgiving man in the world, because, let me tell you, I have done my share of messing up."

"How so?"

I went on to tell her about the abortion I had after Reggie left for college, that it was his child, and that he didn't know about it until we reconciled years later. And I told her about almost losing Reggie due to a stray kiss and the unwanted advances of a very persistent suitor.

"How are things between the two of you now?" she asked.

"Better. Good. And since my panic attack, he's been wonderful, helping more with the baby and everything."

"Okay. Well, I think we've covered enough for today. When we talk next week, we'll discuss the other major relationships in your life."

"Alright," I said as I shook her hand, and then I left and returned home to my family.

Nine

"You Upset Me, Baby"

Tomeka

I walked from the bus stop to the house, and once inside, headed straight to my room and slammed the door behind me. I flopped onto the bed and closed my eyes. I was glad Granny wasn't home yet. She'd gone back to work and had stayed late that day, thank goodness. So I didn't have to worry about her messing with me about homework or chores. I sure didn't feel like hearing her mouth. I was still hurting and sick and upset about Abraham. It had been weeks since I got that break-up letter from him, and he hadn't answered any of the letters I'd sent him.

I missed him so much, and it just made me sick to think that I would have to go on living in that little house in that hick town without the hope of one day being with him. If I'd had someplace else to go, I would've run away ASAP.

"You didn't check the mailbox?" Sharee asked.

I didn't open my eyes as I answered her. "Really? I didn't notice."

"You ain't gotta get all smart with me, Meka. I'm just saying. You been checking that thing like you gon' get a million dollar check or something, and all of a sudden you stopped."

"So?"

"So, I checked it."

"And?"

"And you got a letter from your pen pal, Claudia."

I jumped up from the bed and snatched the envelope from her hand. I felt all nervous and excited at the same time.

"Yeah, I know how excited you get when Claudia writes you," Sharee said, her arms folded over her chest.

I stared down at the envelope and said, "Yeah, thanks."

"Mm-hmm. You want me to leave?"

"Yeah." I looked up at her. "*Please.*"

"You gay now?" she asked, snapping me out of my letter shock and happiness.

"What?!"

"I mean, you always so happy about that girl writing you. So I figured you must be gay now."

I rolled my eyes. "No. She's just a friend. Now get out, Sharee!" I shoved her a little towards the door.

"Okay, okay, fine. But I still say you gay."

"Whatever!" I shouted as I closed the door behind her.

I hurried to the desk and sat down and carefully opened the envelope. I unfolded the paper and smiled. Drawn at the top of the page was a huge rose with my name written in fancy letters next to it. I took a deep breath and then began to read the words written in Abraham's handwriting.

Dear Tomeka,

I got your letters. I didn't write back at first because I really meant what I said about not being good enough for you. I still don't think I'm good enough. But I don't like the idea of hurting you. If I hurt you, I am really sorry. You asked in one of your letters if I loved you or if it was all a lie. I do love you, Tomeka. That's the truth.

If it hurts you for us to be apart, then we can be together even if it is through these walls and only on pieces of paper. When I get out of here, I promise to take care of you and to do right by you. I will be glad when I can see you again. Claudia is going to send you a cell phone. Don't worry about sending her any money.

I hope you like the picture. My cellmate, Karossy, drew it. Okay, well, write back soon.

I love you,

Abraham

I smiled so hard that my cheeks hurt. Everything was good again.

Ten

"Information Blues"

Bobbie

"Tell me about your relationship with your parents," Dr. Bradford said as she reached for her pen and held it over her pad.

I cleared my throat before speaking. "Well, I was very close to my father. I got my love of music from him. He always took real good care of me—spoiled me, really. It's been years since he passed, and I still miss him a lot. No one will ever compare to my daddy." I paused and smiled. "But my husband comes close."

Dr. Bradford smiled. "And your mother? How well do you get along with her?"

I sighed. "Well, my mother is another story. Up until a few years ago, we didn't get along at all. For most of my life, I thought my mother hated me. She disliked my career, thought I was throwing my life away."

"What turned your relationship with her around?"

I twisted my mouth and stared at the heavy-set woman for a moment. "When I was in the hospital for alcohol poisoning, she came to see about me. She took me home with her, and I stayed with her and my nieces for a while. During that time, I got to know Mama a lot better. I grew to understand her and her ways. I learned that we weren't all that different after all. "

"But growing up, you two weren't close at all?"

"No, not even a little."

Dr. Bradford was quiet as she jotted down some notes. I sat in silence, my eyes traveling the walls of the room, noting the certificates and colorful artwork. Her office had a calming and inviting feel to it, as did her demeanor. When I turned my attention back to her, she was staring at me.

"Did you say something?" I asked.

"I was just getting ready to ask you a question."

"Okay."

"Who taught you how to be a mother?"

"What? What do you mean 'who taught me'?"

She adjusted in her chair and laid her pen on the desk. "How did you learn to take care of your child?"

I shrugged, not really sure what she meant by the question. I answered it as best I could. "Well, when I was pregnant, I read a lot of books and Reggie and I attended some classes. Oh, and they showed me how to take care of her in the hospital after I had her."

She shook her head. "Okay, I see that you were prepared for basic care needs. But I'm asking who showed you how to nurture her, comfort her, make her feel safe and loved."

"I…"

"Do you think that those things can be learned in a class or a book, Mrs. Darrough?"

"I…I don't know. I guess all of that stuff just comes naturally."

"Did it come naturally for you?"

I slumped back in my seat, suddenly feeling even more flawed than I had when I walked into her office that morning. "No."

"Why do you think that is?"

"Because I'm all screwed up. Always have been, always will be."

"Do you really believe that to be true?"

"It's the only explanation I can come up with."

She jotted something down on her pad. I imagined it was something like: this woman is crazy.

"Do you think the only way a mother knows to care for her child is naturally?" she asked.

Now I was getting confused. "Well, isn't it?"

"Mrs. Darrough, you know how to read, correct?"

I frowned. "Of course I do."

"Were you born with that ability?"

"No." I wanted to add "Were you?" but decided against it. Sometimes I really hated how therapists played the "quiz game" with you. I mean, I *really* hated it.

"How did you learn to read?"

"My kindergarten teacher taught me." I looked up at Dr. Bradford, my frown deepening. "Are you saying someone was supposed to teach me how to love my baby? But didn't you just say I couldn't learn that in a book or a class."

"I did."

"Then what are you getting at?"

"Okay, let me try another illustration."

How about you don't? I thought.

"You're a singer, correct?"

"Yes."

"And you were born with that talent?"

"Yes."

"What about your style of singing or the things you do during your performances? Where did that come from?"

"I listened to and watched other artists and kind of adopted some of their styles, and—wait, I see where you're going with this."

"I'm not going anywhere. My job is to help you to see things more clearly." She leaned forward and rested her elbows on her desk. "So, what is it that you see, Bobbie?"

"I see that the reason I don't know how to love my baby is because I never observed my mother loving me when I was little."

"Okay."

"Okay, now that I know that, how am I going to fix it?"

"One day at a time."

***

"Hey, Mama," I said after Mama answered the phone.

"Hey, Bobbie Ann. Y'all doin' okay up there?"

"We're fine. How are things with you and the girls?"

"They alright." I could tell there was more she wanted to say.

"Tomeka?"

"Tomeka still bein' Tomeka—runnin' hot and cold. Never know what kinda bag dat girl gon' come out of." Mama sighed. "Done got her some Mexican girl for a pen pal. She like writing letters to her, so I guess dat's good. Other than dat, she don't have much ta say. Been playin' sick jus' 'bout every Sunday so she can miss church."

I frowned. "You're *letting* her miss church. Now that's hard to believe."

Mama sighed again. "Ta tell you da truth, Bobbie Ann, I'm jus' old and tired. Been thankin' dat maybe I shoulda never took on tryna raise these girls. Jus' ain't no fight leff' in me."

I sat down on the sofa. "Mama, are you sick again?"

"Naw, I'm fine. Like I said, I'm old and tired. Ain't natural for a woman my age ta be raisin' kids, 'specially teenagers."

"You need a break? Want me to take the girls for a while?"

"Naw, Bobbie. You got yo' own issues ta deal wit'. How thangs goin' wit' dat doctor?"

I closed my eyes, not wanting to discuss my therapy in light of how Mama was feeling. "Therapy is going okay."

"Humph. You sound funny. Y'all musta finally got ta me."

My eyes widened. Was there anything this woman didn't know? "Actually, yes, we talked about you this week."

"So you figured out I'm da' reason you havin' trouble bein' a mother?"

"Mama, I…"

"It's okay. I know I wadnt no kinda mother to you. I ain't gon' make no excuses 'bout it, either. I was wrong. Did da doctor tell ya how ta fix dis?"

"Not really."

"Well, I'ma tell you how we gon' fix it. I'ma pray harder than I done ever prayed befoe'. I'ma pray harder than I did when I was sick. Da Lord gon' fix dis jus' like he gon' fix Tomeka. But you gotta pray, too, Bobbie Ann. All dat therapy is good but it ain't gon' never beat prayer."

I smiled. "Yes, ma'am."

"And here's another thang. I ain't gon' lie. It was hard for me ta take care of Junior when he was a baby, knowin' how I came ta be pregnant wit' him. But you know how I got through it?"

I felt tears welling up in my eyes. "No, ma'am."

"I told myself dat no matter how he got on dis earth, he was mine. God gave him to me ta care for, and God loved him. It'd been a sin for me not ta love him, too. Remember dat. It'd be a sin not ta love dat precious baby girl."

"Yes, ma'am." As soon as the words left my mouth, Faith began to cry.

"I hear her. Now you gone and take care of her. Remember what I told ya'."

"Yes, ma'am. Bye, Mama."

I hung up the phone and ascended the stairs to Faith's room where I took her into my arms and kissed her little forehead. I sat in the rocking chair and closed my eyes as I began to feed her. "Lord, help me to be a better mother. Show me how to love her. Please, Lord. Please, show me how to be her mother." After I finished praying, I hummed an old hymn and cried silent tears.

Eleven

"Sweet Little Angel"

Tomeka

I was deep beneath the covers when I heard the cell phone buzz. I snatched the covers off of me and instead of sitting up, rolled too far and fell to the floor. My leg hurt as I crawled to the desk and grabbed my purse and dug inside for the phone Claudia sent me. My heart felt like it was going to burst when I finally found the phone, but by then, I'd missed the call. I grunted as I stood to my feet and silently prayed Abraham would call back. I knew it was him because he said he'd call at noon on Saturday. It was exactly 12:01 P.M. Besides, no one else even knew I had a phone. I groaned as I sat on the chair and held the phone in my hand. *Please call back. Please call back...*

I shut my eyes tightly and prayed. "God, if you are really up there listening to me, please, please, please make him call back. *Please.*"

The next thing I knew, the phone was buzzing again. I pressed the button and held it to my ear. "H... hello?"

"Hello, Tomeka?"

OMG! It's him! It's him! "Yeah, it's me. Abraham?"

"Yeah. Oh, man. Tomeka, baby, you sound so sweet."

I was so excited that I could've peed on myself right then and there. He sounded so different from the boys at my school. He sounded all grown up and sexy! "Thank you."

"Oh, Tomeka. I'm so glad to finally get to talk to you. When you didn't answer I thought you'd changed your mind. I thought you didn't want to talk to me."

"No, I was sleep. I'm sorry."

"It's alright. I just got a couple of minutes, though. Can you talk?"

"Yeah. I can talk. My granny and my sister are gone to town. I played sick so I could stay here and get your call."

"Oh, okay. I hate you gotta lie and stuff."

"It's okay."

"I just wanted to tell you I love you. I can't wait 'til I get out of here and can talk to you face-to-face. I just found out I'm up for parole in a couple of months."

"Really?! That's great, Abraham!"

"Yeah. Hey, say my name again. I like the way you say it."

I giggled. "What?"

"Same my name again, baby."

"Abraham."

"Ah, man. I love you, Tomeka. Write me tonight, okay? I'll call you next Saturday. I love you."

"Okay. I love you, too, Abraham."

We hung up and I sat in the chair and replayed our conversation in my head over and over again.

***

Dear Tomeka,

I loved talking to you today. I had imagined what your voice would sound like a bunch of times and now that I've heard it, I think I love you even more. You sounded so good. You sounded just like an angel. That's what you are to me, you know? You're my angel. Having you in my life makes me a better man. I promise that when I get out of here and we can finally be together, I will make you happy.

I've got to go, baby. I know I'll be dreaming about you tonight.

I love you,

Abraham

Twelve

"Easy"

Bobbie

I raced into the house and up the stairs and, as soon as I made it to Faith's room, began hurling apologies at Sis. Purifoy. "I am so sorry. My appointment ran a little late and then the traffic was horrible and I know what a favor you are doing us by keeping Faith for us. I do not want to take your kindness for granted in any way."

She smiled warmly and as she laid a sleeping Faith in her crib said, "I told you, I don't mind at all. It gets me out of the house and this little girl is no trouble at all. It's my pleasure to get to spend time with her. I have grandchildren, but I hardly ever get to see them."

I returned her smile. "I bet you spoil those grandbabies of yours, don't you?"

She picked up her purse from the changing table and slid the strap over her shoulder. "I sure do try. They know when they see me they are in for a treat. I cook up all of their favorite food and feed them until they are full as ticks." She paused and chuckled. "My granddaughter, Ashley, she's seven and she just loves my caramel cake. I think if I let her, she'd eat the whole thing by herself. Of course my grandson, Blake, would have a fit if he didn't get a piece."

I chuckled. "That must be some good cake, then. You'll have to let me taste some of the next one you bake."

"Well, I don't usually do too much baking unless I know my grands are coming for a visit. But for you I can make an exception."

"Oh, no, ma'am. Don't go to any trouble for me. Will you please let me give you a little something for keeping Faith? I want to at least replace the gas you used coming over here."

She held up her hand. "No. This is my pastor's family; I wouldn't dream of taking a dime from you."

"*Assistant pastor*, Sis. Purifoy. And it's the least I can do."

She chuckled. "Well, as far as I'm concerned, your husband *should* be the pastor. But let me hush my mouth." She looked down at Faith in her crib. "No, dear. I can't accept a thing for keeping this little doll." She sighed. "She reminds me of my own daughter."

"You have a daughter, too? I didn't know that."

She laughed lightly. "Oh…well, yes, I have one girl. Bridgett. She's the baby of the family. " She paused and then shook her head. "That was a lifetime ago. They're all grown and long gone now. In their thirties and got families of their own."

I frowned. "Then you must've been really young when you had them. I didn't think you were a day over forty." Okay, maybe that was an embellishment of the truth, but she did look younger than she let on.

She swatted my arm. "Oh, you hush. I know I look my age, and that's fine with me. I count it a blessing to still be here. Well, let me head on back home."

I walked her down the stairs to the front door then out to her car. "Well, next time, I'm bringing Faith to you. That way at least you won't have to fight the traffic to get back home."

"That's up to you. Either way, I'll see you next week."

I smiled. "No, ma'am. You'll see me at church."

She giggled as she unlocked her car door. "That's right. Bye, dear heart."

"Bye," I said and waved as she backed out of the driveway. As soon as I stepped back into the house my cell phone rang.

"Hello?" I answered.

"Hey, baby. You make it home okay? How was your session?" It was Reggie.

"It was good. The doctor thinks I can reduce my sessions to one per month after next week."

"You feeling…better?" he asked cautiously.

"I'm *much* better. Now that I understand my feelings stem from my own childhood and my relationship with my mother, I feel *one hundred percent* better. I really believe I can do this—be a mother, I mean."

"Of course you can. You were born to do it."

I smiled. "You always know just the right thing to say to me."

"I always tell the truth. The truth can't be nothing but right, baby.

I heard the front door open and watched as my gorgeous husband walked into the house. I really didn't understand how after knowing this man for most of my life, he could still make my heart flutter. He walked over to me with the phone still to his ear and kissed me softly.

"Mm, now that was a nice greeting," I said.

Reggie grinned. "Is the little one asleep, because there's much more where that came from."

"She's sleep for now. We better get started, though. She might wake up any minute."

He laid his phone down and began to shed his clothes right there in the living room. "You ain't said nothing but a word." His phone began to ring. He checked the screen and then silenced it.

"Who was that?" I asked as he began to help me out of my clothes.

"No one important enough to stop this."

Thirteen

"My Love Is Here To Stay"

Tomeka

"I'm going for a walk!" I yelled to Granny as I headed out the door.

"You done finished yo' chores?" she called back.

"Yes, ma'am."

"Well, don't be gone long."

"I won't," I said as I closed the door behind me.

I walked down the driveway and headed towards the church. I walked behind the church and took the path into the woods to a place Aunt Bobbie Ann once showed me. She said it was her and Uncle Reggie's "spot." I sat on a log and hoped I would be able to get a cell phone signal out there. I'd been lucky that Abraham's first call had come through.

I stared out at the spring as water bubbled to the surface and made ripples over and over again. I held the phone tightly in my hand, feeling excited and anxious and hopeful all at the same time. When it began to buzz, I jumped up from the log.

"H…hello?"

"Tomeka? Hey, baby. It's Abraham."

I sat back down on the log. "Hey, Abraham."

"Hey…man, you sound even better than last time. Damn, I wish I could talk to you face-to-face, you know?"

"I do, too," I said with a big smile on my face. If this was what love felt like, I never wanted it to end.

"What's your middle name?"

"Huh? Oh. It's Sharnay."

"Tomeka Sharnay Brooks. Beautiful—just like you."

I giggled. "Thank you. What's your middle name?"

"My full name is Abraham Juan Rios. I was named after my grandfather and uncle."

"I like it."

"I like *you*."

I was smiling so hard my cheeks were beginning to hurt. "I like you, too. I *love* you."

"I love you, and I can't wait to be with you. I'll wait no matter how long it takes. Will you?"

"I'll wait forever," I said softly.

"It'll be worth it, baby. Look, I gotta go. You coming to see your dad next week?"

"I think so."

"Okay. Write soon, baby. I love you."

"I'll write you tonight. I love you, too, Abraham."

I ended the call and sat on the log for a few more minutes, daydreaming about the future. About how it would feel to kiss and hug Abraham. I'd never kissed a boy before. Never even hugged one. There just weren't any boys at my school that I liked. I guessed that was because I liked older guys like Abraham. *My Abraham.*

I sighed as I closed my eyes and replayed his words in my head. *"I love you and I can't wait to be with you."*

I couldn't wait to be with him, either.

***

Dear Abraham,

Did you get my other letter? I hope so. Well, I've been thinking about you all week, so I decided to write again. I hope you don't mind.

I just wanted you to know that I love the way your voice sounds. I love to hear you say you love me. I love the way you say my name. No one else says it like you do. I'm so glad we're together even though we can't really be together right now. I love you so much.

I was thinking about what I said about praying and God awhile back, and now I'm thinking that maybe you're right. Maybe he does hear prayers, because when you broke up with me, I prayed for us to get back together and we did. I'm going to pray for you to get your parole and for us to find a way to be together. I meant what I said. I can wait forever, but I really want to be with you as soon as possible. I want to be there when you go home.

Well, I better go. See you soon, I hope.

Love,

Tomeka Sharnay Brooks

Fourteen

"Highway 80 Blues"

Bobbie

We had just dropped Faith off at Sis. Purifoy's house and were on our way to visit Junior. It had been more than a month since our last visit and for the first time, I felt like I would miss Faith. In the past I'd been relieved to leave her behind—sad, but true. This time, I found myself wanting to hold and kiss her as Reggie sped down the highway. This time, I craved my baby's presence, tried to remember her scent. And at that moment, I realized that I *did* love her and that I had loved her all along.

The realization brought tears to my eyes. I quickly swiped at them and smiled. I loved her. *I really loved her.*

Reggie's phone rang. He checked the screen, frowned slightly, and then silenced it.

"Who was that?" I asked, my voice sounding small in my own ears.

"A telemarketer." He glanced over at me. "You okay, baby?"

I smiled through my tears. "Never better. I just can't wait to get back home so I can cuddle my baby in my arms."

He smiled. "Me, either." He placed his hand on my thigh and squeezed. "Did you know you're the best mother and wife in the world?"

"I know I'm the *luckiest* mother and wife in the world. I love you and Faith so much, Reggie."

"I bet we love you more."

I twisted around in my seat and peaked at my grinning nieces. "What're you two cheesing about?" I asked.

Sharee giggled and shrugged.

"You and Uncle Reggie," Tomeka said. "I hope me and my husband are just like you guys."

I frowned a little. "Husband? You got a boyfriend, Meka?"

"She better not," Reggie interjected.

It was Tomeka's turn to giggle. "No, but there's a boy I like."

"Who? Tariq Waters? Ewwww!" Sharee said.

"No, dummy! I don't like that boy!" Tomeka shrieked.

"Well, he sho' likes you!"

"No he don't!"

"Well, whoever he is, he better be careful or else your Uncle Reggie is gonna have to hurt him," Reggie said, peering at Tomeka in the rearview mirror.

"He's really nice, Uncle Reggie," Tomeka offered.

"He better be," Reggie said as he returned his attention to the road ahead.

I turned back around in my seat in time for Reggie to give me a little wink. He was being lighthearted, but I knew he loved Tomeka and Sharee as much as I did, and he was very protective of them. I hoped that Tomeka would be careful with this boy. I made a mental note to talk to her later on and try to find out more about this young man.

***

I really hated visiting Junior in that place. I mean, I really, *really* hated it. There is nothing worse than seeing someone you love locked up behind bars. Yes, me and Junior had had our ups and downs. He'd hurt our family over and over again, but he was still my brother, and I would always love him. But as much as I hated his current situation, I knew it was what he deserved. After all, I was the one who called the police and reported his confessed murder of Nora Lee.

I did it because it was the right thing to do and because as the mother of his children and as a human being in general, Nora Lee deserved justice. But it was still hard seeing him in that uniform and those heavy shoes. It was hard seeing the defeated look in his eyes, the look that all of the inmates shared—a look of fear mixed with despair and desperation. I really did hate it.

Going through the security checks and signing in at the desk had become routine. Walking into that big room and picking a table to sit at had become commonplace. And I hated the whole experience more for my nieces than I did for myself. Along with coping with the death of their mother—at the hands of their father—they also had to visit their father in prison. I prayed that the effects of what was going on wouldn't be long-lasting. I prayed that they would find a way to get past the mess Junior had made of his life and move on to become great women.

We all sat at the table and awaited Junior's arrival. I observed the girls and noticed that both of them were watching the door, both anticipating seeing their father. It seemed that they loved him despite his flaws. I hoped Faith would be so forgiving of me, because I wasn't perfect and knew I never would be.

Junior finally appeared and a huge grin spread across his handsome face. He quickly made his way over to the table and shook Reggie's hand. He then gave me a warm hug and kissed my cheek and just as he did every visit, whispered, "Thank you, sis", in my ear.

I smiled and whispered back, "You're welcome", like I did every visit.

Sharee stood and hugged him without hesitation. Tomeka was another story. For some reason, her eyes were still glued to the doorway. It was as if she was ignoring Junior on purpose.

"Meka, can I have a hug?" Junior asked softly.

Tomeka turned and looked at Junior. "Huh? Oh, yeah, okay." She seemed preoccupied and as she stood to hug him, I noticed her eyes were still on the door. It was almost as if she was looking for someone— someone other than her father. But how could that be? Who else could

Tomeka have possibly known in that prison?

She acted strangely the entire visit and barely paid attention to any of us at the table. Junior tried to talk to her, but she had very little to say. She kept surveying the room, her eyes darting towards the door over and over again. This was weird even for Tomeka. By the time we were ready to leave, she looked near tears. I tried to talk to her on the ride home but got the silent treatment. What was going on with her?

Fifteen

"How Blue Can You Get"

Tomeka

I sat in the backseat of Uncle Reggie's truck trying not to cry. None of them showed up. Not Abraham or his sister or his mother. *None of them.* I nibbled at my fingernails as I tried to figure out what happened. When I snuck into Aunt Bobbie Ann and Uncle Reggie's basement and took Abraham's phone call the night before, all he'd talked about was how he couldn't wait to see me. So, what happened? Why hadn't they shown up? Had something happened to one of them?

I was so worried that I didn't even hear Aunt Bobbie Ann talking to me. Sharee poked me in the side and gave me a crazy look and that's when I realized she had asked me a question. But I still didn't answer her. I knew that if I opened my mouth, I was going to bust out crying and then when she asked me why, I was going to have to think up some lie about my daddy or something, and I just didn't feel like it. So I just sat back there and stared out the window and when we made it back to the house, I ran inside to the room me and Sharee always slept in and closed the door.

I lay on my face and closed my eyes and finally let myself cry. I had wanted to see him so badly, had waited so many weeks. I just didn't understand what happened. My heart was aching and my head was hurting and when I heard the knock at the door, I just wanted to scream and tell whoever it was to leave me alone. But I didn't. I didn't say anything at all.

I heard the door open and then I heard footsteps on the hardwood floor.

"Tomeka? " It was Aunt Bobbie Ann. Well, at least it wasn't Super-Sleuth Sharee. I wasn't in the mood for her.

"Tomeka," she repeated. "You alright?"

I nodded, my face still pressed to the bed.

"Do you want to talk?"

"No," I said into the sheets.

Aunt Bobbie Ann sighed. "You know me and Uncle Reggie love you, right?"

"Yes, ma'am," I said as I continued to cry.

"And you know you can tell me anything? *Anything*, Tomeka."

"I know."

"Okay, well, I'ma get started on dinner. Uncle Reggie's gone to get the baby. We're gonna eat a little while after he gets back."

"Okay."

She left and I sat up in the bed and wiped my cheeks. I sat there for a minute and then dug in my purse and pulled out the phone. It had been on silent, so I didn't notice the call when it came. I rushed to the door and locked it and listened to the voice message.

"Tomeka? Tomeka, baby. I'm so sorry I didn't get to see you today. My mom and Claudia had a wreck on the way here. They're okay, but they had to miss the visit. I'm sorry, baby. I'm so sorry. I love you. I'ma try to call you again later, okay? Bye."

I closed my eyes and breathed a sigh of relief as I replayed the message. After I listened to it a third time, the phone lit up with a new call flashing across the screen. *Abraham.*

"H...hello? Abraham?" I answered eagerly.

"Yes, angel. It's me. Did you get my message? I'm so sorry, baby," he replied.

"It's...it's okay."

"No, it's not. You sound upset. I hate letting you down. You know I'd never let you down on purpose, right?"

"I know. I was upset, but now I'm okay. It wasn't your fault. I'm glad Claudia and your mom are okay."

"Yeah, me, too."

Knock, knock!

"Unlock the door, Meka!" Sharee yelled.

I groaned. "I gotta go, Abraham. Write me tonight, okay?"

"I will, mi amor. I love you."

"Love you, too."

I ended the call and turned the phone off before sliding it back into my purse. I checked my face in the dresser mirror and was smiling when I opened the door for Sharee. "You ain't got to yell," I said.

"Oh, so now you smiling? You are so crazy, Meka. I swear you are special," Sharee said as she walked over to the bed and began changing her clothes.

I tried to stop smiling but I couldn't. "So I gotta be crazy 'cause I'm smiling?"

She rolled her eyes. "No, you gotta be crazy 'cause you *crazy*. I promise you need help. Uncle Reggie is back. I'm gonna go play with Faith, *weirdo*."

I rolled my own eyes and sat on the side of the bed thinking about Abraham.

Sixteen

"When The Blues Comes Knockin'"

Bobbie

I was leaving my final therapy session and I felt good. I'd miss being able to bend Dr. Bradford's ear, but I was glad she thought I'd made enough progress to be released.

I smiled at the thought of kissing and holding my little girl once I picked her up from Sis. Purifoy's. I was glad I wouldn't have to impose on her anymore, though she looked a little sad when I told her this was my last therapy session. I assured her I would still need her to keep Faith from time to time, especially when I took the girls to see Junior. That seemed to lift her spirits.

As I sat in the bumper-to-bumper traffic, my mind drifted to Tomeka. I was really concerned about her behavior during the last visit. So much so that after discussing her with Reggie, we decided to put more space between the visits to the prison. Reggie and I agreed that they were taking more of a toll on her than we'd realized. I hadn't told Mama about my concerns yet. Every time we talked about Tomeka, it seemed that Mama expressed less and less concern about the situation. It was beginning to remind me of how she reacted to me when I was Tomeka's age. It was almost as if she didn't care at all. As if she was just biding her time until Tomeka was eighteen and out of the house.

Now that I had my head on straight, I could play a more active role in the girls' lives, maybe even let them spend the summer with me and Reggie and give Mama a much-needed break. Summer break was only a week or so away, and though I needed to take my music on the road again, I would be sure to make time to do things with the girls and maybe instead of bothering Sis. Purifoy so much, the girls could watch Faith sometimes.

I was mapping out things in my head when my cell phone rang. It was Reggie. I answered the phone with, "Hey, baby."

"Well, hey yourself. I'm on my way home from work. Where are you?"

"Stuck in traffic. Lord only knows when I'll make it to Sis. Purifoy's to get Faith."

"I'm closer to her house, so I'll get her. You just head home and get naked."

I laughed. "Um…why would I get naked?"

"Because it should be Faith's nap time when we get home and I'm tryna make another baby."

I laughed louder. "You are so silly. You sure you want to keep making babies with a lunatic like me?"

"Baby, by now you should know I love you, crazy and all. And I definitely love making babies with you."

"Okay, well, see you at home."

"Naked?"

"Yes, silly, *naked*. And Sis. Purifoy is supposed to be giving us a cake she baked so don't forget it."

"Oh, man, cake and you in the nude. This is gonna be a good night!"

I smiled all the way home.

I made it home, rushed upstairs to take a quick shower, and was toweling off when I heard the phone ring. It was Reggie again. I accepted the call and greeted him with, "Where you at? I'm naked and waiting for you."

"Um, Bobbie. Where is the baby?"

"What? I thought you were picking her up?"

"Yeah, well, I'm here at Sis. Purifoy's house but she doesn't have the baby. She says you never dropped her off."

I dropped the towel. My heart began to race. "What? Of course I dropped her off. I dropped her off like I do every Thursday. I dropped her off, and then I went to my appointment. What is she talking about? Faith is there."

"Hold on, baby. She wants to speak to you," Reggie said.

The next voice I heard was Sis. Purifoy's. "Dear heart, don't you remember calling and telling me you didn't need me to keep her today? She's not here because you didn't bring her."

"Sis. Purifoy, what is going on? You know I brought her. I put her in your arms and you kissed her cheek. Why are you lying?"

"Honey, are you feeling okay?"

"I'm fine! I know what I did! I *know* I gave her to you. Now, where is she?!"

"There's no need to yell, dear. I'm sure Brother Reggie will help you figure this out. I hope you find that precious baby soon."

"Find her?! She's with you! *You* have her!" I screamed into the phone.

"Bobbie, it's me," Reggie said. "Calm down, okay? She says the baby's not here. She seems to be telling the truth."

"What?! You believe her? You believe *her* over *me*?!"

"No, I just...I'm worried about Faith."

"Faith is in that damn woman's house, Reggie, because that's where I *took* her. Just stay there. I'm on my way."

"On your way to do what?"

"I'm gonna make that old bat let me search her house. I don't know what the hell she's trying to pull, but I'ma show you that she's lying and I'm gonna make her give me my baby back. Then I'm gonna kick her old ass."

And with that I hurriedly dressed, ran out to my car, and broke all speed limits on my way across town to her house.

Seventeen

"Your Love Makes Me Feel Good"

Tomeka

Dear Tomeka,

I have a surprise for you, but I can't tell you what it is right now. I'm excited about it, though. I hope it will make you happy. I hope it will make things better for us. I'm so sorry I didn't get to see you at visitation. I want to see you so bad, but worse than that, I want to touch you. I want to kiss you and to hold you. I think about it all the time. I wonder how you will feel in my arms. You are so beautiful. Sometimes I sit and stare at the picture you sent me the other week. I stare at your beautiful face, the face of an angel. My angel.

I really hope you share my feelings. I hope you miss and want me as much as I miss and want you. And when we get to be together, I hope we never break up. I don't ever want to be apart again.

I love you,

Abraham

I held the letter to my chest and took my regular seat on the ground next to the mailbox. I watched the sun set and pretended that Abraham was with me, holding me, kissing me. When I closed my eyes I could almost feel him there. I could almost feel his lips on mine. I could—

"Tomeka! Granny said you need to get in here and finish washing these dishes!" Sharee's voice brought me back to reality. Abraham wasn't there with me. He was still in prison, and I was stuck in that hick town with my stupid little sister and crazy grandmother. I stood to my feet and kicked at loose gravel all the way up the driveway back to the house. I rolled my eyes at Sharee as I shoved past her into the house. I stomped to the kitchen and began slamming dishes into the sink.

"I don't know what yo' problem is, girly. Butchu bet' not break not nann one uh my dishes. You hear me?" Granny said.

I sighed and closed my eyes. "Yes, ma'am."

Eighteen

"I Done Lost My Baby"

Bobbie

I raced into Sis. Purifoy's driveway so fast that I almost rammed into the back of my own husband's vehicle. I snatched the door open, jumped out of the car, and ran right up to the front door. I banged on it, adrenaline fueling my every move. Sis. Purifoy opened the door with this you-poor-crazy-little-thing look on her face. And behind her stood Reggie with confusion written all over *his* face.

"Where is my baby?!" I shouted.

"Well, only you know the answer to that, dear heart," she answered calmly.

I stepped closer to her and glanced at Reggie. "Don't 'dear heart' me. I brought my baby here this afternoon and dropped her off and you know it."

"No, sweetheart, you didn't. You called and told me you no longer needed me to keep her on Thursdays, remember?"

"Yes, and I was standing right here handing her to you when I told you that! I told you that I wouldn't need you after *today*."

She shook her head. "Well, if that's true, why isn't she here?"

"Because she *is* here!"

"Look, you're welcome to come in and look for her, but your husband already did, and he didn't find her because she's not here."

I pushed past her. "I'll take you up on that offer."

I stalked through the house shouting Faith's name. That way, if she was somewhere asleep, maybe I could wake her up. I searched and yelled her name for the better part of an hour before real panic set in. She wasn't in that house. What had Sis. Purifoy done with her or...*to* her?

I walked back into the living room where both Reggie and Sis. Purifoy stood waiting for me. "Where. Is. She?" I said evenly.

"Sugar—"

"Look, old lady, I *know* I brought her here. You have obviously done something with her. WHERE IS SHE??!!"

Reggie reached for my arm. "Bobbie—"

I turned and looked at him. "No, Reggie. She had her. I brought her here; I dressed her in that yellow dress that your secretary bought her. I packed her diaper bag. I put her in her car seat, and I brought her *here*. I know I did! I am *not* crazy."

"We just...we just need to find her. Could you have forgotten and left her at home, Bobbie?" Reggie asked calmly. Too calmly—like he was talking to an escaped mental patient.

I frowned. "You don't believe me, Reggie?"

"I don't...I don't know what to believe. All I know is that Faith is not here."

"Fine then, Reggie. You think I'm lying? Go check the house and see if I left her."

He just stood there and stared at me.

"Go!" I shouted.

Reggie gave Sis. Purifoy an apologetic look. "Come with me," he said.

"What? You think I'ma hurt this old bat? I'm not. As a matter of fact, I'm going to let the police handle her."

I followed Reggie outside and climbed into my car. He tapped on my window, and I opened the door. "Are you gonna follow me home?" he asked.

I shook my head. "No, I'm gonna call the police and wait for them to get here in case she tries to leave."

"O…okay. I'll call you when I get to the house."

"Yeah…okay. Call me when you don't find her." I shut the door and dialed 911.

***

I sat in my car clutching my phone as I watched the police officer knock on Vera Purifoy's front door. I'd just finished telling him what was going on. Hopefully, she would have sense enough to tell the police the truth and give me my baby back. Crazy old lady.

I watched as she opened the door and invited the officer in, then I dialed Reggie's number.

"Hello?" he said, sounding weird.

"She ain't there, right?" I said.

"No, Bobbie. I didn't find the baby here."

I sighed. Sis. Purifoy was so convincing that for a second there I thought I actually *was* losing my mind. "*Now* do you believe me? This old lady is out of her mind. I just pray Faith is somewhere safe. I don't know what I'll do to her if she hurts my baby."

Reggie was silent.

"Reggie, you still there?"

"Yes...um, Bobbie?"

"Yeah? What is it?"

"I didn't find Faith, but I did find something else."

"Baby, you don't sound right. What is it?"

"I found her dress—the yellow one you said you dressed her in. And I found the diaper bag. It's all packed up and sitting right here in her room."

"What?! No, no, no! That can't be. I know...*I know* I brought her here. I know I did."

"Bobbie, are you still over at Sis. Purifoy's house?"

"Yes, but I'm coming home. I need to see for myself. I…"

"Bobbie—"

There was a knock on my window. I looked up to see the police officer peering down at me with a stern look on his face.

Nineteen

"Down the Dirt Road Blues"

Tomeka

Dear Abraham,

I don't know when I'll get to write you again. I'm leaving with my grandmother to go to Houston. My little cousin, Faith, is missing. The police think maybe my Aunt Bobbie Ann did something to her because she was real depressed and stuff. I just don't believe that. Aunt Bobbie Ann is the best person in the world. I just don't believe she'd do anything to hurt her own baby.

I'm so upset right now but I wanted you to know why I can't write for a while. School is almost out so Granny doesn't care about us missing these last few days. I don't know how long we're going to be in Houston. I guess until they find the baby. I hope they find her soon. I've got to go now, but I'll try to find a way to answer your call on Saturday.

I love you,

Tomeka

Sharee ran into our room as I shoved the letter into an envelope.

"Meka, come on! Granny already out there in the car. We gon' miss our bus if you don't stop messing around!"

"I'm coming!" I said as I licked the envelope.

"You and them letters. You act like the world gon' end if you don't write Claudia. I swear y'all gay."

I walked out of the room, ignoring her last statement. I ran past Granny's car to the mailbox and shoved the letter inside then ran back to the car and slid into the backseat. "Sorry it took me so long, Granny."

Granny looked at me in the rearview mirror. "Jus' buckle up. We ain't got time for no foolishness right now. We need ta get ta da bus station."

Then Granny drove faster than I'd ever seen her drive before. She was really scared and so was I. I loved Aunt Bobbie Ann and little Faith. I really didn't want anything bad to happen to either one of them. I closed my eyes and thought about what Abraham said about prayer.

"What you doing?" Sharee asked, noticing that my lips were moving but I wasn't saying anything out loud.

I looked over at her. "Praying."

She grabbed my hand and closed her eyes, too.

***

The bus ride wasn't all that long, but that was probably because we were all too worried to notice. We took a taxi to Aunt Bobbie Ann's house and when we got there, there were two police cars in the driveway. Uncle Reggie met us in the driveway and hugged all of us. He looked so worried.

"Where Bobbie?" Granny asked.

"Inside. The police are talking to her again. They were here half the night asking questions, and they came back this morning asking the same questions. I don't know what to do, Ms. Mae. She's my wife and I want to believe her, but she was so depressed and I don't know…"

Granny grabbed Uncle Reggie's hand. "You know Bobbie Ann better than anyone else in dis world. Deep down in yo' soul, do you thank she coulda done somethin' like dis?"

"In my soul? No, I don't."

"Neither do I. We gotta stand wit' her. Okay?"

Uncle Reggie nodded. "I know. You're right. I just…I'm worried about my little girl." Then he began to cry. And so did me and Sharee.

Granny hugged him. "You listen here. Dat baby is fine. I done prayed, and I know she fine. We gon' get her back. You hear me? We gon' get her back."

Uncle Reggie nodded and wiped his face. "Y'all come on inside."

Twenty

"Police Man Blues"

Bobbie

"Okay, now, let's go over this one more time, Mrs. Darrough. What exactly happened yesterday afternoon?" the officer asked.

I sighed heavily, frustration crowding every inch of my mind. "I've told you this three times already. You are wasting time. That insane old lady has my baby somewhere. You need to be questioning her, not me!"

"We've already spoken with her. And as you know, she says you never came to her house yesterday. You never took the baby to her."

"She is *lying*. How many times do I have to tell you this?!"

The officer just sat there and stared at me.

"Look, you are wasting precious hours here! I thought the first 48 hours were crucial to an investigation. You've already wasted almost 24 hours!"

"A *homicide* investigation, but your baby is not a homicide victim, *is she?*"

"What the hell?! I didn't kill my own child. That crazy-ass old lady has her!"

"Mrs. Darrough, your cooperation would make our work much easier."

I dropped my head. "Okay, fine. I will tell you what I've told you a million times already. I bathed Faith, dressed her in a yellow dress, put her little socks and shoes on her, packed her diaper bag, carried her out to the car, strapped her into the car seat, drove across town to Vera Purifoy's house, carried her to the front door, and placed her in that woman's arms. We had a little light conversation, and then I left for my appointment."

"Your appointment with your psychiatrist?"

"Yes."

"Where Mrs. Purifoy says you were being treated for postpartum depression."

I hesitated, dropped my eyes, then said, "Yes, but the doctor released me yesterday. I'm...I'm fine. "

"Okay, Mrs. Darrough, how do you explain your daughter's clothes and the diaper bag being found in her room?"

"I don't know." I thought for a moment, then added, "She babysat here on several occasions, and she knew where the spare key was. And she knew the code to the gate. She wouldn't even have had to stop at the guard shack to get in. Maybe she snuck in here and left the dress and the bag."

"Why would she do that?"

"To make me look crazy."

"Okay. Where is the spare key? Is it missing?"

"I'll check," Reggie said.

I hadn't even noticed that he was back in the house. He headed to the kitchen where we kept the spare key in a drawer. Another officer followed him. I noticed my mother and nieces standing just outside the living room. I was glad to see them, but that gladness didn't even put a dent in the worry and despair I was feeling.

A few seconds later, Reggie and the other officer returned—Reggie held up the spare key. Everyone's eyes were on me.

I shook my head. "She could've made a copy."

The officer who'd been interrogating me sighed. "I think I have all I need for now." He stood to leave.

I frowned. "Wait! Don't you want a picture of her for the media or something?"

The officer hesitated and then said. "Yes, of course."

Reggie grabbed a framed photo of Faith from the mantle and handed it to the officer.

"We'll be in touch," the officer said. And then both officers left.

Mama and the girls rushed to me. Mama sat down next to me and grasped my hand. My eyes welled up with tears. "They're not going to do anything to find her. They've got their suspect. And it's me."

"No, I believe they gon' see da truth and they gon' look for her. You gotta believe dat, too, Bobbie Ann," Mama said.

I looked over at Reggie who stood across the room, a look of confusion and doubt on his face. I looked at the confused, scared expressions my nieces wore. And then I looked over at the family photo that hung on the wall—a photo of me and Reggie and Faith. I remembered how anxious I had felt about taking care of her. I remembered how I hated waking up at night to feed or change her. Had I brought this on us? Was it really my fault she was gone? Was it possible that I'd really done something to my own child?

I stood to my feet and shook my head. "No!" I screamed to no one in particular. "No! No! No!" I ran from the living room to the foyer where I grabbed my keys and ran out to my car. Reggie was hot on my heels as I jumped in my car and screeched out of the driveway.

Twenty-One

"The Things That I Used To Do"

Bobbie

Five years.

Five years, one month, and ten days to be exact. That's how long it had been since I'd had a drink, since I'd felt the comforting burn of liquor as it slid down my throat. And as I sat there staring at the half-empty glass of brown heaven that sat on the bar before me, I felt like I'd been reunited with an old friend. I picked up the glass and watched the liquid swirl around and around. I smiled as I held it up to my nose and breathed in its scent. As I brought it to my lips, I felt someone sit down on the stool next to mine.

"Celebrating?" a smooth baritone voice asked.

I downed the remains of my drink, let out a little grunt, and said, "Married. Not interested."

"Aw, now. I just wanted to buy you another drink so you can keep your little party going."

I turned and looked at the stranger. He was tall, dark, thin, and relatively handsome. When you have Reggie Darrough for a husband, handsomeness is always relative. As far as I was concerned, there was no match for Reggie's looks.

The stranger was dressed in a sleek, pin-striped suit with a canary yellow shirt underneath. His matching pin-striped tie was tied in an intricate knot. He smelled wonderful and if I had been drunk enough to forget I was married and madly in love with my husband, I would've considered getting a room upstairs. He was smiling widely, drinking in my body with his eyes. I turned and stared at my empty glass. "Bartender, another one, please," I slurred.

"On me," the stranger said as he slid a hundred dollar bill across the bar. "And I'll have whatever beautiful here is having."

The bartender refilled my drink, and I turned to my drink fairy and said, "Thanks."

"You're welcome. I'm Martin, by the way. "

"Hmm, really?" I replied with a tad bit of sarcasm.

"Yeah. What's your name?"

"It's better if you don't know."

"Woman of mystery, eh? I can dig it. So what are you celebrating?"

"Not celebrating. I'm actually in mourning."

"Oh, damn, I'm sorry. Who'd you lose?"

"I didn't. Somebody took something...*someone* from me. My child."

"That's messed up."

"As my mama would say, damn sho' is. Minus the damn, that is."

"So, mystery lady, you come here often?"

I laughed. "Damn, you don't get out much, do you? You really need to work on your pick-up lines."

He chuckled. "Dang, you gotta call me out like that?"

I shrugged. "If the shoe fits…"

"Okay, tell me this: What kind of fool would let a woman like you sit in a hotel bar full of men alone like this?"

"Better, but you still need work."

He laughed again. "You didn't answer the question."

"How do you even know I have a man?"

He pointed to my left ring finger.

"Aren't you observant?"

"I'm a P.I. I get paid well to be observant. Plus, you already told me you were married."

I nodded. "Oh, yeah. Shoot, I must be drunk. Getting forgetful."

"Still didn't answer my question. Trouble in paradise, mystery lady?"

I downed the rest of my drink. That made five drinks for me and I was definitely out of practice because the next thing I knew, I was sliding off of the bar stool. The last thing I remember was feeling someone grab me.

Twenty-Two

"Soon As The Weather Breaks"

Tomeka

"Where are you now?" Abraham asked.

I adjusted the cell phone on my ear. "In my aunt's basement. It's gotten real crazy up in here. My aunt left yesterday morning, and we haven't seen or heard from her since. My little cousin is still missing, and the police still think my aunt had something to do with it."

"That's messed up, baby. You must be worried sick."

"I am. I wish I could be with you right now."

"Didn't you say your aunt lives in Houston?"

"Yeah."

"Look, I was gonna wait and surprise you, but I guess I can go on and tell you. They moved my parole hearing up. It's in a couple of days. If everything goes well, I could be home in a week or so. This joint is so overcrowded; they're almost pushing folks out."

"Oh my God! For real, Abraham?! Are you serious?!"

"Yes. I'm glad you're excited. And if you're still in Houston when I get out, we could probably hook up since that's where my mom stays. I'll have to parole out to her house."

"That would be awesome, Abraham!"

"Meka?! Meka, you down here?" Who else but Sharee?

"I gotta go. Call me some time tomorrow if you can," I whispered into the phone.

"Okay, love you," Abraham said.

"Love you, too."

I quickly ended the call and shoved the phone into the pocket of my pants. I watched as Sharee walked down the stairs and over to the couch where I was sitting.

"Why you down here in the dark?"

I shrugged.

"Ooo, wee! You getting crazier and crazier."

"What do you want, Sharee?"

"Granny looking for you. It's lunch time."

I stood and followed her up the stairs. "Aunt Bobbie Ann back?"

Sharee shook her head. "Naw. Uncle Reggie still out looking for her. They still ain't found the baby, either. You think Aunt Bobbie Ann did something to her for real?"

I frowned. "No! I think that old lady did something. People are crazy, you know?"

"Yeah, I know. I live with a crazy person, remember?"

"Whatever. You don't know nothing about me, Sharee."

She stopped just outside the kitchen and turned and looked at me. "Then tell me. You used to tell me everything. Now everything with you is a big secret."

I looked at her for a moment, and she actually looked kind of sad. I really did want to tell someone about Abraham, but I was scared. After all, he was a grown man—a grown man who was in prison. I was closer to Sharee than anyone else in the world, but I knew that not even she would understand our love.

"I can't," I said softly.

"Fine. I don't care anyway."

We were both silent as we entered the kitchen and sat down at the table. Granny looked worried when she took both of our hands and began to say grace.

Twenty-Three

"Morning Sun Blues"

Bobbie

I bolted upright in the bed, confused by the scene that surrounded me. I wasn't at home. I was somewhere else. A hotel, maybe? I could hear the shower running. Someone else was here. Reggie?

I swung my feet around and sat up on the side of the bed. I was wearing jeans and a t-shirt. *I fell asleep in my clothes?* I stood from the bed and walked over to the mirror that hung on the wall. My eyes were swollen, and I looked horrible. As I ran my fingers through my dreadlocks, the memories of the previous night came rushing back—the drinking, the man at the bar, him carrying me up to this room. *Did we—did I...*

I searched the room with my eyes and quickly found my shoes and purse. I grabbed them and headed for the door, but before I could make my exit, the man, *Martin*, emerged from the bathroom with a towel wrapped around his waist. Though he was thin, his chest and abs were defined. Through sober eyes, Martin was more attractive than I'd first believed.

"You just gonna sneak out on me, mystery lady? Now, that's just rude," he said with a grin on his face.

"Um, I don't know what happened here last night, but I was drunk and you need to know that it never would've happened if I was sober. I'm married and I love my husband and I'd never do anything like this if I was in my right mind, but so much has been going on and my baby is missing and no one will believe me when I tell them what happened and—"

He held up his hand. "Whoa, whoa…look, nothing happened. You passed out and I brought you up here to my room so you could sleep it off."

I rubbed my hand back and forth across my forehead, trying to calm the throbbing that seemed to intensify with each beat of my heart. "Are you sure?"

He tilted his head to the side and eyed me from head to toe. "Believe me, beautiful. If we'd done anything, *anything at all*, I would remember even if I was drunk *and* high."

I released a sigh of relief. "*Thank God.*" I looked up at him. "No offense."

"None taken. Hey, let me get you some coffee and something to eat before you leave."

I stood by the door and shook my head. "No, I really need to go. I'm sure my husband is looking for me."

"I gave you my bed and slept on the floor." He pointed to a pillow and a blanket lying on the floor next to the bed. "The least you can do is have breakfast or brunch, or whatever you call it at this time of day, with me."

I sighed and closed my eyes. "Okay, I guess I do need to put something on my stomach." I shook my head. "I can't believe I got drunk."

He nodded towards a small table near the window. "Have a seat."

"Could you put on some clothes?"

"Sure thing, mystery lady, if that's what you really want." He gave me a wink before grabbing his clothes and disappearing into the bathroom.

Thirty minutes later, we were both seated at the table eating a light brunch. I drained my coffee cup and smiled at him. "Thank you for…everything. I really appreciate it."

"No problem, mystery lady."

"It's Bobbie."

"I know. I searched your purse."

My eyes widened.

"I didn't take anything. I'm a P.I., remember? Snooping is second nature."

I shook my head.

"Well, Bobbie, how long were you sober?"

"How—"

He raised his eyebrows and nodded towards my purse. "I noticed the AA keychain."

"Five years."

"I was once sober for ten."

"You fell off the wagon last night, too?"

"No, beautiful. I fell off months ago."

"I'm sorry."

He shrugged. "Yeah, well, some people are just born to mess up, huh?"

"I used to think I was."

"I saw your baby's picture, too. Beautiful little girl."

I nodded, stared down at the remnants of my meal, and began to cry.

"I'm sorry. I didn't mean to upset you," he said.

"You didn't. It's just…" More tears. I sobbed loudly.

Martin placed his hand over mine and rubbed it gently. When I was finished crying for that moment, he said, "If you tell me what happened, maybe I can help you."

"I don't see how you can," I said as I took the tissue he offered to me.

"How many times I gotta tell you? I'm a P.I., baby."

I sighed deeply. "Okay." As he refilled my coffee, I began to tell him about Faith's disappearance. I told him *everything*—about Sis. Purifoy and her lies and the clothes and diaper bag showing up at the house. I ended with, "The police think that either I'm crazy or I'm lying or both. But I'm not, Martin. That woman is lying and I pray to God that she hasn't harmed my child."

Martin stared at me for a moment. "I believe you."

Finally, *someone* believed me.

"And you really think you can help?" I asked.

"I *know* I can. It's what I do best, gorgeous. Write down this lady's address. I'll start with her."

"Okay, and I can write you a check for the fees. How much?" I asked as I wrote down Sis. Purifoy's address and my cell phone number.

"No charge."

I looked up at him with a creased brow. "But—"

"Look, this big-time lawyer is paying me a lot to dig up some dirt on one of his client's wives. That's why I'm here. I don't need your money. Anyway, I love helping out beautiful, sexy, damsels in distress."

I smiled and handed him the paper. "Thank you, Martin." I stood to leave.

"No problem, Bobbie. I'll be in touch as soon as I can."

I hesitated and then hugged him. "Thanks, again."

He smiled down at me. "Talk to you, later."

I left his room and boarded the elevator. When I made it to the lobby, I saw my husband standing at the front desk. I stood there for a moment staring at him, knowing that I had worried him by disappearing. I slowly walked over to him and gently placed my hand on his back.

"Reggie," I said softly.

He turned around and faced me and relief covered his handsome face. "Oh, baby," he whispered as he pulled me into a tight hug. "I was so worried." He gripped me tighter. "I tried to call but your phone just kept going straight to voicemail. I was *so worried…*"

I closed my eyes. "I know. I'm so sorry."

He released me and then held my face in his hands. "Are you…are you okay?"

I nodded. "I am now. Can you just take me home? We can come back for my car later."

He kissed my forehead and then pulled me into his arms again. "Okay. You need to check out first?"

I shook my head. "No, I…uh…I already did."

Once we were inside the car and on our way home I looked over at him and asked, "Any word on Faith?"

"No, not yet. But I've been praying and we've just got to trust God with her. We're going to get her back, Bobbie. I really believe that."

"So you believe me, now? You believe that I took her to Sis. Purifoy's?"

He glanced over at me. "Yes, I do."

I let out a breath. "Thank God." I paused then added, "How'd you find me?"

He gave me a small smile. "Same way you found me that time in Magnolia. I checked all of the credit card transactions, heard the hotel's name, and drove straight over there. I was having a hell of a time trying to convince that clerk to give me your room number."

"Sorry." What I didn't say was that there was no room number to give since I'd never checked into a room myself. I'd only used the credit card at the bar.

He reached over and grasped my hand. "It's okay. I found you. That's all that matters. Please don't run away again. We're in this together, baby."

"Okay, I won't. Um, Reggie?"

"Yeah, baby?"

I stared out the windshield. "I...I got drunk last night."

Reggie sighed. "Oh, baby..."

"I know. All those years, all of the meetings and hard work down the drain," I said as I began to cry.

Reggie pulled over on the side of the road and reached for me. I leaned across the console and rested against him. "It's alright. We're gonna get through this. I love you, Bobbie. I love you so much."

"I love you, too."

Twenty-Four

"Worried Dreamer"

Tomeka

When Aunt Bobbie Ann finally made it back home, she and Uncle Reggie looked so sad and so tired. I really wished there was something I could do besides sit around and wait. Me and Sharee helped Granny cook and clean, but that just didn't seem like enough. I would've given anything to bring my little cousin back home. I needed to do something to help. Something that really counted.

I thought about what Abraham had written in one of his letters: *Praying is good, Tomeka. God loves us. He loves you. Don't forget that.*

I kneeled beside the bed and closed my eyes. "Dear Lord, it's me, Tomeka. But I guess you already know it's me. And I guess you already know about my cousin, Faith. Please watch over her, Lord, and please keep her safe, wherever she is. Please help Aunt Bobbie Ann and Uncle Reggie. They are so worried about her. Please help them to feel better. And please help my Granny, too, because she's worried. I know she talks to you all the time, but I wanted to tell you about her, too. And lastly, Lord, can you help Abraham to get out of jail? He's really a good person and he deserves to be free. Okay. I guess that's it. In Jesus' name, amen."

I opened my eyes and stood from the bed and when I turned around, I saw Sharee standing behind me.

"Who is Abraham?" she asked.

"None of your business! Dang, I can even pray in peace!" I stormed out of the room and headed downstairs.

Granny was on her knees in the living room praying again. I could hear her saying, "Lawd ham-mercy. Ham-mercy, Master! Ham-mercy!"

I sure hoped Abraham was right. I hoped that all of the praying we were all doing would do some good.

***

I was sitting on Aunt Bobbie Ann's back porch, watching some birds fly from tree to tree, when I felt my phone vibrate in my pocket. I stood up, glanced back at the patio doors to be sure that no one was watching me, and walked towards the fence. I leaned against it and answered the call. "Hello?"

"Tomeka, baby?"

My heart jumped in my chest. "Yeah, Abraham?"

"Yeah. Hey, my hearing is in a little bit, and I wanted to call you since you're my good luck charm."

I smiled. "I'm glad you called. Good luck, Abraham. I've been praying for you."

"My luck has been good ever since I met you, baby. Keep praying, angel."

I looked up and saw Aunt Bobbie Ann step out onto the back porch. I inched along the fence until I was behind the pool house. "Hey, I gotta go. I love you so much, Abraham. I'll love you no matter what they decide," I whispered.

"Thank you, baby. I'll call you after it's over."

"Okay. Bye, Abraham."

"Bye. I love you. Talk to you soon."

Twenty-Five

"Got To Find My Baby"

Bobbie

When my phone rang, I was sitting next to Reggie in our bedroom. He was making calls, coordinating the ongoing search party of church members and friends. The number on my screen was unfamiliar to me, so I figured it was either a wrong number or Martin. I let it roll to voice mail as Reggie hung up his phone.

"I'm gonna call and see if I can get an update from the police. Who was that calling you?" he asked.

I wasn't sure if it was a good time to bring up Martin since I wasn't sure if he had or would find anything to help us, and I didn't want to get Reggie's hopes up for nothing. I'd put him through enough with my disappearing act.

"Probably a telemarketer. I didn't recognize the number. How's the search going? I feel like I should be doing more to help," I said.

"Deacon Yancy has recruited most of the men from the church plus a bunch of his friends to comb Sis. Purifoy's neighborhood. Hopefully they'll find someone who saw you drop Faith off or saw her with Faith.

And the best thing for you to do is stay here. I don't need to have to bail you out for assaulting that old lady."

"Cause you know I would."

"Yeah, you definitely would."

I smiled. "Look, I'ma head downstairs so you can make the rest of your calls in peace. Love you."

"Love you, too, baby. I'll let you know if there's any news from the police."

"Okay."

As I walked out of the room, Reggie's phone began to ring. I hesitated and watched as he picked it up, checked the screen, silenced it, and shook his head. Okay, I might've been a lush, but I was far from a fool. Clyde Morgan, my ex-husband, had given me a good education on phantom phone calls and what they meant. Something was going on, but I had more urgent things to think about at the moment. I needed to find my baby. I would have to deal with Reggie and his little phone buddy later.

I hurried down the stairs, through the living room, and out the patio doors to the back porch and then hit the button to call the number back.

"Martin Miller," said the voice on the other end.

"Miller? I guess I didn't catch your last name before," I replied.

"Yep, Martin Luther Miller."

"Is that seriously your name?"

"Yes, gorgeous, it is. Look, I got some info for you."

"Already?"

"Yep. Your lady wasn't home when I made it over here, so I dropped in on her neighbor. Turns out she left town a couple of days ago, the day after your little girl went missing. The neighbor says Mrs. Purifoy asked her to watch the house for her. Said she'd be gone indefinitely."

"Did the neighbor see a baby with her?"

"No, she didn't."

I sighed and took a seat in one of the patio chairs. "I just don't understand. Where in the world could she be hiding her?"

"I don't know, but I'm waiting for her landlord right now. She's gonna let me into the house so I can check things out."

My ears perked up at hearing that. "Really? Don't you need a warrant or something to do that?"

"Beautiful, the only warrant I need is Mr. Ben Franklin. You'd be amazed at the access he and a couple of his twin brothers can get you."

"I bet. You sure this won't mess up the police investigation?"

"Well, from where I'm standing, there *ain't* no investigation. Look, I know what I'm doing. I'm not going to touch anything. I'll let you know what I find out. Try not to worry. I'ma find your little girl."

"Thank you, Martin."

"It's all good, gorgeous. Later."

"Okay, bye."

I sat there for a moment, deep in thought. I was startled when Tomeka appeared at the base of the steps. "Meka! Where did you come from? You scared me to death!"

"I'm sorry, Auntie," she said with a sheepish look on her face.

"What you doing out here all by yourself?"

She shrugged and her eyes darted from my face to the ground. "I don't...I don't know. I was just walking around. Thinking about swimming."

I frowned. "Oh, well, I'm sorry we've still got the pool covered up from the winter. Maybe we can open it up after we get Faith back." As soon as I said her name, tears I'd been fighting for hours threatened to break free.

"Okay. Aunt Bobbie Ann, you okay? Is there anything I can do?"

I smiled at her. "Can you pray for Faith?"

"Yes, ma'am. I've already been praying for her."

"That's all I can ask you to do. It's the *best* thing you can do."

She walked over to me, bent over, and wrapped her arms around me. "I love you, Auntie."

"I love you, too, Meka."

My phone began to ring. I recognized the number as Martin's. "Meka, would you go and check on Mama? She's been so worried."

"Yes, ma'am," she said as she slipped back into the house through the patio doors.

"Hello?" I said softly.

"Gorgeous? It's me. I need to talk to you ASAP."

"Well, talk."

"No, baby. I need to talk to you in person. Got something to show you."

"Um…okay. Uh, I'm at home right now. Can you come to my house?"

"Sure. What's the address?"

"8008 Cherry Ridge Lane. It's in the Enchanted Forest Subdivision. I'll call the guard shack and let them know you're coming. And Martin?"

"Yeah, sexy?"

"My husband is here. Please don't refer to me as sexy or gorgeous or anything like that, okay?"

"Gotcha, beauti—I mean, Ms. Bobbie."

"Okay, see you in a few."

"Alright."

Twenty-Six

"Things Ain't Right"

Bobbie

I sat in the living room with my family surrounding me, took a deep breath, and began to speak. "There's a man coming over in a minute...a private investigator. He's found out some information about Mrs. Purifoy."

Reggie straightened his posture and with a slight frown said, "A P.I.? When...what—"

"I...uh, met him at the bar the other night. I bent his ear, and he offered to help us find Faith—free of charge."

"Good Samaritan, huh? Good deal. Wish I thought of hiring a P.I. 'cause the cops ain't worth a damn right now," Reggie said. "Excuse my language, everyone."

"They got they mind set dat Bobbie got somethin' ta do wit' dis. They gon' feel real stupid when they find out they wrong," Mama said.

"I hope things go that way, Mama," I said softly. "Back to Martin— that's his name. He's says he's found something we need to see."

"Okay, well, I can't wait to see what he found out," Reggie said.

About twenty minutes later, the doorbell rang. I hopped up from the couch, and nearly tripped over Reggie's feet as I hurried from the living room. "I'll get it!" I called as I made my way to the foyer. I opened the door and smiled at Martin who looked like he'd just stepped off of the cover of *GQ Magazine*.

He smiled at me and whispered. "Damn, your husband is a lucky man."

I rolled my eyes. "I thought this was a business call."

"It is."

"Well, come on. Everyone's in the living room."

"Everyone?"

"My family."

Martin eyed the walls as I led him from the foyer to the living room. "Whose gold albums?" he asked.

"Mine. And one of them is platinum—not gold."

He stopped in his tracks. "Well, damn. You a star? And the police dragging their feet like this?"

"They think I'm a deranged, baby-hiding star. Plus I'm only a mid-level star and I'm black and so is my baby. You know how that goes."

"Humph," he said. "We're just gonna have to fix all of that."

We entered the living room and I made the introductions, then we all sat down and Martin pulled an iPad from his satchel. "First, let me reassure you, Mr. Darrough, that I am going to do everything in my power to find your baby," he said.

Reggie nodded. "Any help you can give us is appreciated."

"No problem. First, I want to know what you two know about Vera Purifoy."

Reggie shrugged and looked over at me as he began to speak. "She belongs to the church we attend. I'm an associate pastor there. Um, I think she joined shortly after we did."

I frowned slightly. "She did? I thought she'd been there for years."

Reggie shook his head. "No, I remember when she joined. She said she'd just moved to town and was looking for a church home."

I nodded, surprised at this information. For some reason I had just assumed she had lived in Houston much longer than that.

"What about her family? Do you know anything about them?"

I glanced at Reggie. "Um, she told me she had five kids. They're all grown, of course, and she has some grandchildren. I'm not sure how many, though. From the way she talked, none of them live here in the city," I said.

Martin nodded, swiped his hand across the iPad a few times, and then laid it on the coffee table in front of us. "I took these pictures in her house just a few minutes ago."

I looked at the images before me, but did not trust my own eyes. There was picture after picture of me and Reggie and Faith attached to a bulletin board in some room.

Alarm shrouded Reggie's face as he looked over at me then turned to Martin and said, "What is all of this? She's…she's been stalking us?"

"It would appear that she has," Martin replied.

"Where…where did you find this? I looked in every room in that house, including the basement, and I didn't see this," I said.

"In the back of one of her closets—the one in her bedroom. You probably checked it and didn't notice its true size. At first glance, it looks very small, but it's actually pretty deep."

"But why? Why us? Why would she be stalking *us*? Why would she take *our* baby?" I asked.

"Well, Ms. Bobbie, that's the trillion dollar question, isn't it?" He leaned forward. "I've got my assistant back home working on trying to get some background information on Purifoy, since she's able to access all of the software and databases on the computer in my office."

Reggie nodded. "Okay."

"I have another question for the two of you."

"Yes?" Reggie and I said almost in unison.

"What have you been doing to find your daughter?"

"Some of the church members have been posting and handing out flyers with Faith's picture on them and canvasing Sis. Purifoy's neighborhood. I sent in some information and they featured our story on the news the first night Faith was missing. I called in and did a radio interview this morning. And I've been calling around, but the police said to just stay by the phone, so that's mostly what we've been doing," Reggie said.

Martin was quiet for a moment. "Well, I have an assignment for the two of you."

"What is it?" I asked.

"Ms. Bobbie, you're a celebrity, and judging from the basketball trophies over on that mantle, you aren't too shabby, either, Mr. Darrough. The police force is dragging their feet when they should be working overtime to find your daughter. The two of you need to take a more proactive role in this."

"Okay, how?" Reggie queried.

"I want you to call and schedule some interviews. And I'm not talking about calling the local news stations. No one watches the news enough for it to matter. You need to call one of those tabloid gossip shows. You know, the kind that loves to slant things and blow them out of proportion. You need to do an interview on one of those shows and lay it on thick about how the police aren't doing enough to find your baby. I need you two to play the hurt, broken, disgruntled parents thing to the hilt, but I know that won't be hard to do. I know you guys must be worried sick.

"Talk about how this woman took your child and lied about it and the police won't do anything to her. Demand that they search her house thoroughly so that they will find this." He pointed to the pictures. "You're going to have to embarrass the police into doing their job and at the same time, it will antagonize them. They're going to push back and probably make accusations against you to save face. But, at least it will get them in gear. I know this has been hard for the two of you. I know you are worried and overwhelmed right now. I know you've been trusting the police to do something. But you're going to have to *make* them do something."

I nodded and felt like a light bulb had gone off in my head. Reggie and I had been so upset about the situation that we'd been letting precious time slip by. Martin was right; we had to demand that something be done.

"Do you two get what I'm saying?"

"Loud and clear. We're gonna get right on this," Reggie replied.

Martin stood from his seat. Reggie stood and shook his hand. "We really appreciate this."

"No problem. I'll be in touch as soon as I hear from my assistant."

Reggie walked Martin to the door, and I grabbed my phone and began making phone calls.

Twenty-Seven

"This I Swear"

Tomeka

I sat in the corner of the living room and watched as Aunt Bobbie Ann wiped tears from her eyes. Uncle Reggie held her hand as she told the story of Faith's disappearance for the sixth time in two days. At that moment, Katie Wilkes was sitting in the living room listening to her. Yes, *the* Katie Wilkes of The Katie Wilkes Show. I knew Aunt Bobbie Ann had to be tired of saying the same thing over and over again, but she never skipped a beat. She told the story through her tears. She was so strong.

Granny and Sharee were in the kitchen cooking dinner. Granny just about lived in that kitchen. Some people drink and smoke, and Granny cooked. I wasn't complaining, though. If there was one thing my Granny could do, it was burn in the kitchen. She was in there cooking fried pork chops, collard greens, and candied yams. I couldn't wait for dinnertime.

As I sat and watched them wrap up the interview, I felt my cell phone vibrate in my pocket. I held my hand to the outside of my pocket as my heart sped up. I stood from the chair and quietly walked behind the cameras and out the door. I peeped in the kitchen at Granny and Sharee who both stood over the stove, their backs to the doorway. Then I eased up the staircase and into the bedroom, closing and locking the door behind me. I sat on the side of the bed and hoped Abraham would call me right back. I hadn't heard from him since his parole hearing, and I was a nervous wreck.

I didn't have to wait long. The phone began to vibrate again, and I quickly pressed the button and placed it to my ear. "H...hello?"

"Hey, Meka?"

"Yeah, how did it go?"

"Well...I did the best I could do, you know? I told them I was reformed and that I've never even looked at drugs since I got arrested. I told them that I had someone new in my life—someone I love very much and that I was ready to start a new life with her, and..."

I held my hand to my chest and closed my eyes. "And..."

"And I got my parole, baby!"

"Oh, Abraham! I am so happy for you...for us! I can't believe it!"

"Me, either. Oh, man, angel. I can't wait to get to see you."

"When do you get to leave?"

"They're talking about the end of the week. Like I said before, it's really overcrowded in here, so they're pushing folks out the door. Hey, how about this? How about I don't call you again until I'm free? That way, when you see the call, you'll know I'm out of here."

I was smiling so hard that my cheeks were beginning to burn. "Okay. Hurry!"

He laughed. "I wish I *could* hurry. I love you so much, Meka. Thank you for taking a chance on me and letting me into your life. You won't regret it."

"I love you, too. I can't wait for us to be together. I really can't."

"Okay, I gotta go. Um…Meka?"

"Yeah?"

"I've got something I need to ask you when I see you, okay?"

"Okay."

"Bye, angel."

"Bye."

***

Dear Abraham,

We just talked on the phone and I am so excited about you getting your parole. I am so happy that soon we will get to see each other and touch each other.

I wanted to write you this letter because there is so much I need to say to you, but sometimes I feel kind of shy, and we are never on the phone long enough for me to tell you anyway.

I just want to thank you for choosing me to love. I know you said you had a girlfriend before you got locked up, and I know you didn't decide to break up with her until after we got together. I know that probably was hard for you to do, breaking up with her after you had been with her for so long. You said I wouldn't regret giving you a chance. Well, you won't regret choosing me, either. I promise to do everything I can to make you happy. I will be good to you, and I will love you with all of my heart, forever. Once we are together, I don't ever want to be apart again.

Love,

Tomeka

Twenty-Eight

"Have Mercy"

Bobbie

Reggie and I sat in our bedroom and watched the last of the interviews on the TV. It seemed that Martin's advice had paid off. The hotline Reggie and I had set up was receiving a steady stream of tips and offers to help with the search. I prayed that at least one of the calls would pay off.

Reggie clutched my hand tightly as the interview ended and Katie Wilkes signed off. He breathed a sigh and said, "You were great, baby. I wish I'd said more, but I just get so nervous in front of those cameras."

I squeezed his hand. "You said enough. I hope *I* said enough. I hope something that we said prompts someone to come forward."

Reggie' phone rang. He walked across the room and picked it up. I waited for him to silence it and make up some lie about who it was, but instead, he looked over at me and said, "It's the police."

I rushed over to him as he accepted the call and put it on speakerphone. "Hello?" he answered.

"Mr. Darrough? This is Officer Pettus with the Houston PD. Just wanted you to know that we've received several tips over the past few hours, and we're following up on every one of them. If we get anything concrete regarding your daughter's disappearance, we will call you ASAP."

"We appreciate that, Officer," Reggie said.

"We're also mounting a comprehensive search for Vera Purifoy, and we're consulting with the FBI. Someone should be over later today to put a tap on your phone just in case there's a ransom demand."

"Great. We'll look forward to it." He hung up and smiled at me. "Looks like your boy, Martin, was right. All of those interviews lit a fire under them."

I nodded. "Thank God."

As if on cue, my phone began to ring. I looked up at Reggie. "It's Martin."

"Hello," I said, answering the call.

"Hey, Ms. Bobbie. You busy?"

"No, not at all."

"Well, I'm headed your way. Got something to show you guys."

"Okay, we'll be waiting for you."

Martin must not have been that far away when he called, because what felt like seconds later, our doorbell rang. Reggie let him in and once we were all seated in the living room, he dropped a bomb on us.

He held up a brown envelope and said, "This is the report my assistant worked up on Vera Purifoy and faxed over to me." He pulled out a sheet of paper and laid it on the coffee table in front of us. It was a photocopy of a driver's license. The photo was a younger version of Sis. Purifoy, but the name didn't match.

"Who is Francine Walker?" Reggie asked, mimicking my thoughts

"That is Vera Purifoy's real name. Francine Walker, forty-five years-old. Never been married. No kids."

With wide eyes I said, "Vera Purifoy is an alias? But, why?"

Martin shrugged. "I would assume it was to keep you two from finding out her true identity."

"I still don't know who she is," I said and then glanced over at Reggie who looked like he'd just seen a ghost. "Do you?"

Reggie continued staring at the paper, then looked up at me and absently said, "What? Uh, no...I don't know her."

Martin nodded. "Well, I've got her phone records from the past couple of months. You guys check these out; let me know if any names or numbers ring a bell." He placed the printouts in front of us and I began to slowly canvas the names and numbers with my eyes.

Page after page, column after column, row after row, name after name, number after number—nothing rang a bell, not one. I glanced over at the page Reggie was checking then I looked up at his face. I watched as his expression changed from one of concentration to one of shock. He picked up the page, his hand shook as he brought it closer to his face.

"I…I know this name," he said.

I scooted closer to him, trying to get a better view of the paper. "Which one?" I asked.

Reggie looked from me to Martin as he pointed to the name. "Caprice Taylor. She…she's my ex-wife."

I sprung up from the couch. "What? She's been calling your ex-wife? Why…how does she even know her?"

Reggie looked up at me then quickly dropped his gaze. "I think Sis. Purifoy or Walker or whoever is Caprice's aunt. I thought I recognized the name on the driver's license but at first I wasn't sure. If I remember correctly, they were very close."

I frowned. "Why didn't you recognize her before now if they so were close?" I asked.

"I never met her. They just talked on the phone a lot."

"You think she stole our baby for Caprice?" I asked Reggie.

"I…I don't know."

"Well, that doesn't make sense, anyway. I mean, you haven't even spoken to her since before we got married."

Reggie was silent.

"*Have you?*"

He looked over at Martin. "Can you give us a minute?"

Martin nodded. "Um, sure. I'll be in the kitchen. Smells like someone is doing some serious cooking up in there."

"Thanks," Reggie said.

I folded my arms across my chest. "Reggie, what is going on?"

"Sit down, baby," he replied.

"No, tell me what's going on."

He reached up and rested his hand on my arm. "Please, sit down."

I sat down and scooted to the far end of the sofa. "Tell me."

"Um...I haven't exactly been truthful about Caprice."

"Really? I'm so surprised," I said as I rolled my eyes.

"Baby, don't act like that. Hear me out. I heard you out when you needed me to."

"Oh, so now we're bringing up the past, huh? I thought you'd forgiven me for the whole Dr. Cagle thing."

"I have. Just listen to what I have to say, *please*."

"*Talk*, Reggie."

"Um, right after we got married, Caprice called and said she'd heard about the wedding. She said she was calling to wish us well and to tell me about her kids. I always like hearing about them because no matter how things went down between us, I still care about her kids."

I nodded. "Mm-hmm."

"Anyway, she'd call from time to time, every three months or so. When the whole thing happened with Dr. Cagle, she happened to call and I just needed someone to talk to, Bobbie. I was hurt, and I wasn't sure how far things had gone between you and him...and I wasn't sure about Faith. I mean, like I said before, in my heart I always knew she was mine, but there were these doubts in the back of mind up until the day she was born."

I turned my head and stared at the fireplace. "What happened to remove the doubts? The fact that she came out with brown skin? Or the fact that she looks just like you?"

He shrugged. "It was just something I felt the first time I held her—a bond. I knew she was mine."

"I see."

"Anyway, for a while, Caprice and I would talk a couple of times a week. Sometimes we'd meet for lunch. And then one day, about two weeks before you had the baby, she invited me to her place for lunch—"

"Wait, Caprice lives *here*? In Houston?"

Reggie's eyes focused on everything except for my face. "Yes. She's lived here longer than we have."

"Wow," I said as I shook my head.

"Bobbie, I'm sorry for keeping this from you. We were just friends, but I didn't think you'd understand that."

"You're right. I *don't* understand it."

Reggie sighed. "Look, she invited me over to her place for lunch and she kissed me and one thing led to another and—"

I jumped up. "You better not be getting ready to say what I *think* you're getting ready to say!"

He stood to face me. "I'm sorry, baby."

"You're *sorry*? You're sorry!?" I shrieked.

He placed both of his hands on my arms. I jerked away from him. "Bobbie…Bobbie, *please*. Please listen to me. We didn't really do anything. I mean, she did something to me, but I didn't touch her. I swear I didn't."

"But *she* touched *you*, right?!"

"Yes, but I made her stop, before…*you know*."

I shook my head and fought the desire to kick my husband where he'd been "touched".

"Baby, can't you see? I was confused and it was an accident. I thought she was someone I could trust."

"An accident? Now, that's a new one," I scoffed. "And how the hell did you think you could trust the woman that cheated on you and had a baby by another man while you were married to her? I mean, no matter what you *thought* about me, you had documented proof of what *she* did."

"I don't know what I was thinking. Bobbie…look, that day, after we did what we did, I told her we couldn't talk anymore. I haven't answered any of her phone calls since."

"Mm-hmm, and all of those telemarketer calls? They were from her, weren't they?"

"Y…yeah, they were. I was going to change my number, but I never got around to it."

"Plus, you weren't sure how to explain to me why you were changing it, huh?"

"Yeah."

"Do you think she could've had something to do with Faith's disappearance?"

"I don't know. Maybe. Her last few messages sounded pretty desperate. She was basically begging me to call, said she'd do anything to be in my life again."

I stood and stared at him, and I guess the exhaustion of looking for my baby, fighting accusations that I'd done something to her, and hearing what Reggie had just told me was too much for me. I was too tired to argue, too worn-out to scream. I moved closer to him and softly said, "If that witch has my baby, I'm going to kill her, and then I'm leaving you."

"Bobbie! Please don't do this. I love you!"

I left the living room and as I entered the foyer, grabbed my purse and keys and headed towards the door.

Before I could open it, I was met by Martin. "You okay, Ms. Bobbie?"

I shook my head and turned to face him. "Hell, call me sexy if you want to. It's not like it matters anymore."

"That bad?"

"Worse."

He moved closer to me. "Look, I didn't mean to start any trouble."

I glanced towards Reggie who was walking towards us. "You didn't. I appreciate what you're doing to help us."

"Bobbie, come back and talk to me," Reggie said once he reached us.

"Go to hell, Reggie!" I yelled, finally losing my composure.

"Whoa, okay…um, I think I'll just leave now…" Martin said under his breath.

Before he could make his exit, Mama and the girls came rushing into the foyer. "Lawd, what's goin' on?" Mama asked.

"Ask Reggie," I said.

Reggie shook his head. "Bobbie, don't do this. Don't do this to us, baby, *please*."

"I didn't do anything! *You* did!"

Knock knock.

"Who the hell is it?!" I yelled through the door.

"Police," a voice answered.

Twenty-Nine

"Cross My Heart"

Bobbie

We all stood frozen. I looked from Mama to Reggie to Martin. Then I opened the door and said, "Yes?"

"Mrs. Darrough?" the officer said

"Yes," I replied.

"I'm Officer Darwin. I would like for you to accompany me to the police station for further questioning regarding the disappearance of your daughter."

I opened my mouth to speak, but Martin moved between me and the officer. "I am Mrs. Darrough's attorney. She has already been questioned *extensively*."

"Yes, sir. I realize that, but new evidence has been uncovered and my superiors would like for her to come in for more questioning."

"Is there a warrant for my client's arrest?" Martin asked.

The officer shook his head. "No, not as of right now."

"Then she is not going anywhere."

The officer hesitated and then said, "Very well, then."

The officer turned to leave and Martin shut the door behind him.

"You're a lawyer?" I asked.

"Hell, no. But he didn't know that. Look, this is playing out just like I knew it would."

Reggie nodded. "They're retaliating due to all of the press by moving in on Bobbie."

"Yes," Martin said. "I don't know what evidence they have, but I don't think it implicates our Vera Purifoy. And that's who they should be dogging—not you, Ms. Bobbie. Hell, they're probably bluffing anyway. Most likely, they just want to get you down there and polygraph you. I'm surprised they haven't already done that anyway. But then again, they've been dropping the ball all over this investigation. Anyway, they'll probably want to do a more intensive interrogation, too. You know, get in your face and try to trip you up."

"They can polygraph me all they want, and they can't trip me up because I'm telling the truth. What do you think we should do, Martin?" I asked.

"If we're going to keep you out of jail, we need to find your daughter and we need to find her within the next twenty-four hours. Because the next time the cops come knocking at your door, they *will* have a warrant. I'm going to head over to your ex-wife's, Mr. Darrough. Either she has the baby or she knows where she is."

"I'm coming with you," Reggie said.

Martin shook his head. "No, I don't think that's a good idea."

Reggie wasn't backing down. "Look, if she cares about me like she says she does, I might be our best bet at getting information from her."

Martin sighed. "Okay, fine. Let's go."

"I'm going, too," I interjected.

Reggie shook his head. "No, you stay here."

I stepped closer to him. "*No*, I'm going. It's my baby, too."

"Look, you can both go. Ms. Bobbie, it'll probably be best for you to stay in the car, though. She might clam up if she sees you," Martin said.

"Fine, let's go."

Reggie grabbed my arm. "Martin, me and Bobbie will go in my car. You can follow us."

Martin nodded and headed out the door.

Reggie turned to Mama. "We'll be back as soon as we can, Miss Mae."

"Okay, y'all jus' be careful," Mama said.

Once I was captive inside Reggie's car, he started up again. "Will you listen to me now?"

"No."

"Bobbie, *please*."

"Well, damn. I'm here in a confined space with you. Do I really have any choice?"

"Okay, what happened with Caprice was a mistake."

I glared at him. "*Really?*"

"Okay, it was a *big* mistake. And I'll never be able to tell you just how sorry I am. I love you baby. *Only you.*"

I sighed and fixed my eyes on the scenery outside the window.

"I was messed up in the head, baby. I love you, Bobbie. I loved you the whole time I was married to her. I've only ever loved *you*. You know this. You have got to forgive me, baby."

I turned to face him. "I know you love me, Reggie. But you've been lying and sneaking behind my back with your little *friend* our entire marriage. I can't just act like it never happened and forgive you on the spot."

He glanced at me. "Can you ever forgive me?"

"If I don't get my baby back safely, and I find out that Caprice had anything to do with her disappearing, I will hold you personally responsible and no, I will *never* forgive you."

"We'll get her back."

"You better hope so."

We made the rest of the ride in silence. Unanswered questions filled my mind. *Why would she do this? What did she hope to gain by taking my baby? How long had she planned it? Had she hurt my little girl? Was my baby still alive?*

I shut my eyes tightly and began to silently pray as that last question echoed in my mind. She had to be alive. She had to be okay, because if she wasn't, my life was over. There would be no need in going on, would there? How would I ever get over losing her? I closed my eyes tighter, prayed harder, and fought the fear and anxiety that threatened to overtake me.

I had to be strong.

I had to have faith.

I had to believe.

I looked over at Reggie, some of my anger at him subsiding and being replaced by raw dread. "Reggie, I can't live without her," I said softly.

Reggie pulled the car to a stop in the driveway of a neat brick home. The garage door was up revealing a sleek, black Mercedes with a vanity plate that read BLKBUTY.

Reggie reached over and tightly grasped my hand. "You listen to me. I'm going to get our baby back if it's the last thing I do. Do you believe me, Bobbie?"

I looked up at him and saw the determination in his eyes. "Yes, I do."

He leaned over and kissed me on the forehead. "Good. Stay here. I'll be right back."

Reggie stepped out of the car and waited for Martin to park on the street in front of the house and then, together, they approached the house, engaged in a hushed conversation every step of the way.

I watched as Reggie rang the doorbell, waited a few seconds, and then knocked on the fire-engine red door. Then I heard him yell his name. I guess someone had asked him to identify himself. The door flew open and Caprice greeted Reggie with a big smile. But almost instantly, her smile faded. She could see by the look on Reggie's face that he was there for business, not pleasure.

She let Reggie and Martin into the house and I sat there for as long as I could—which amounted to about three minutes. Then I slid out of the car and walked up to the door. I *had* to be in there. I had to know what she knew. I couldn't wait to get some second-hand report from Reggie or Martin. I needed to know in real time what was going on.

I started to knock, but decided to check the door instead. If it was unlocked maybe I could slip inside undetected. Hopefully her kids weren't home at the moment. I tried the knob and sure enough, it was unlocked. I quietly crept inside and shut the door behind me. I could hear voices just off the foyer in what was probably the living room. There was no other noise in the house, so I assumed her children weren't home. I inched along the wall, stood just out of sight next to the living room doorway, and listened.

"Yes, I heard about your baby. It's been all over the news. I've been praying for you," she said. It took all of my strength not to go in there and choke the life out of her.

"Yeah, I've been really worried about her, Caprice," Reggie said.

"I'm sure you have. Is there anything I can do for you, Reg? Anything at all?" Caprice replied.

"Um, as a matter of fact, there is. Uh, my friend Martin here, he's a private detective. He's been checking up on our babysitter, Mrs. Purifoy."

"Oh, really?" she asked. I could just picture her wearing a wide-eyed, innocent expression. I really wanted to hurt her.

"Yes. I know who she really is, Caprice."

"Well, who is she?"

"Your aunt. Your aunt, Francine. But then again, you already knew that, didn't you?"

"Aunt Francine? I haven't talked to her in months. Why would she be posing as someone else?"

"Come on, Caprice. I remember you and her used to talk all the time. You called her so much when we lived in Italy, our phone bill was through the roof."

"Well, that's because I was all the way across the ocean, and I had no one to talk to. I don't talk to her nearly as often since I've moved here."

"So, you're telling us it's a coincidence that your aunt, who lives here in town, used an alias, joined the same church as your ex-husband, and posed as a baby sitter for his child?" Martin asked, echoing my thoughts.

"No, I'm telling *Reggie* that," she said curtly. "You believe me, don't you Reg?"

Reggie sighed heavily. "Look, Caprice, I wish I had time to play around with you, but I don't. My baby, *my only child,* is missing. And if you know something, you need to tell me."

"I'm telling you, Reggie. I don't know anything."

That was it for me. My baby was missing, and I was tired of listening to Reggie play nice with her. I stepped into the doorway and marched over to where Caprice sat on the sofa next to Reggie, her hand covering his, and I exploded. I snatched her up by her hair and screamed, "You know where my baby is and you need to tell me now before I beat the life out of you!"

"Bobbie!" Reggie yelled. "I told you to stay in the car and let me handle this!"

I turned to him and said, "Yeah, well from what I could hear, you weren't handling it very well." I twisted her hair around my hand, tightening my grip. "Where the hell is my baby?!"

"Reggie, make her stop!" she whined.

"He won't be *making* me do a damn thing! You need to tell me what you did with my child, you sick witch!"

"Bobbie, let her go. Let me handle this. *Please*. This is not going to get us anywhere. She's not going to tell you," Reggie said calmly.

"What makes you so sure she'll tell *you*? Sounded to me like she was stalling."

"Because she loves me," he said. He looked at Caprice. "You love me and you'd never do anything to hurt me, would you, Pree?" he asked.

She smiled, then winced, then smiled again. "You haven't called me that in a long time."

"I know. Will you help me, Pree? *Please*?" Reggie rested his hand gently on her arm. I frowned and loosened my grip on her hair. What was going on here?

"I will if she leaves," she said softly, her eyes glued to Reggie.

"Well, I ain't going no—damn—where, b—"

Reggie cut me off. "It's her baby, too, Pree. Don't you think she's worried?"

She nodded as well as she could with my hand in her hair.

"Now, will you tell me what you know, baby?" Reggie asked. My frown deepened. Did he just call her *baby*?

"What did you—" I began, but Reggie held up his hand to silence me.

"Pree, me and her—we're over. I just need to get my baby back. That's all I need to do to move on with my life. Maybe we can start over. But I can't do that without my little girl. Do you understand?"

"Yes," she said with a big sappy smile on her face.

"Bobbie, let her go," Reggie said sternly.

I was so confused by what was going on that I released her without a word. Was this just an act to get her to talk? And if so, was she really falling for it?

I backed away as Reggie took Caprice's hand in his and sat next to her on the sofa. He smiled at her and held her face in his hands. "You okay, Pree?"

She nodded. "Yes."

"Did you tell your aunt to take my little girl?"

She dropped her eyes.

"Tell me and I promise I won't get mad. I just need to know the truth."

"Yes, I did."

I gasped. She actually admitted it?

"Why, Pree?" Reggie asked.

"Because that baby was the only reason you were with her."

"Why did you think that?"

"Well, I just knew it. We were making progress until she had that baby."

"No, Pree. Remember? I had cut things off before Faith was born."

"And you said it was because you were going to be a family. And then you stopped answering my calls, and it just drove me crazy. I knew I had to do something."

I could tell Reggie was struggling to keep his cool. He was just as outraged as I was. "Um, okay, and you told her to make it look like Bobbie did something to her?"

She nodded enthusiastically. "Yes, it made sense since she was having such a hard time taking care of the baby anyway. Plus, that way she would be out of the picture for good in case you got weak and decided to try to stay with her."

"And you thought that would clear the way for us to be together?" he asked.

"Yes. I *knew* it would. And see, you're here. And you just said yourself that you two are over. It worked!"

What a twisted soul! I thought.

"Okay, Pree, tell me this. Is my baby okay?"

"She was the last time I saw her."

I watched as Reggie nodded slowly. His eyes darted towards me then focused on Caprice again. "Okay, when was that?"

"Earlier today. A few hours ago."

"Where's she been all this time?"

"She and Aunt Francine have been staying in some horrible fleabag of a motel across town."

"Where was she the day your aunt took her? We searched her house and couldn't find her."

"She was here with me that day."

"And now? Where is she? Where is my baby?"

She shrugged. "I don't know."

"Oh, hell no! Your crazy ass is going to tell us where my baby is!" I screamed.

Reggie shook his head. His eyes still on Caprice. "Bobbie...Bobbie, let me talk to her. She's going to tell me because she loves me. Right, Pree?"

"I'm telling the truth, Reg. I don't know exactly where she is. Aunt Francine said she was going to get rid of her."

I fell to my knees and began to cry. Martin rushed over to me and helped me back on my feet. Reggie stood from the couch and stared down at Caprice. "What?! What do you mean *'get rid of her?'*" Reggie asked— his voice so small that I barely heard him.

She stood and grabbed his hands. "Oh, no, Reggie. That came out wrong. She knows a couple in Dallas willing to pay a lot of money for a baby. She's on her way there now, but I don't know the address."

I collapsed against Martin and started to breathe again. My baby was still alive.

The tension began to leave Reggie's face as he looked over at Martin. "Did you get that?"

Martin pulled a small voice recorder from the pocket of his jacket. "Every word."

Thirty

"Feel So Bad"

Bobbie

"You recorded me?! Reggie, *you recorded me*?!" Caprice screamed.

Reggie nodded and grabbed both of Caprice's arms. "I'm sorry. I had to. That's the only way the police will believe me. They still think Bobbie had something to do with my baby disappearing."

"Reggie, they are going to put me in jail! My kids won't have a mother. You love my kids. How could you do this?"

I shook my head. Could she even hear herself? Did she realize just how crazy she sounded?

Martin slipped out of the room. I could see him standing just beyond the doorway dialing a number.

"Caprice, it's going to be alright. I'll make sure you get the help you need, okay?" Reggie said softly and then wrapped his arms around the lunatic. "Where are the kids now?"

She rested against him and sobbed loudly. "They're with my mother. She's keeping them for a few weeks this summer. Oh, Reggie!"

"Shh, it's okay. Caprice, can you tell me one more thing?" Reggie said gently.

She nodded against his chest and wrapped her arms around him. I wasn't sure what bothered me more: the fact that she was so crazy or the fact that Reggie seemed to understand her so well.

"Your aunt has belonged to my church for years. Have you had her watching us all of this time?"

"Y-y-yes," she snuffled.

"Did you pay her or something? Why would she do that?"

She looked up at Reggie, her face wet, smeared mascara trailing down her cheeks. "Because she loved me, and she wanted to help me. Reg, I was so depressed after we got divorced, I tried to commit suicide. After your mother died and we reconnected, I thought for sure we would get back together and when we didn't, it was like losing you all over again. I just couldn't take it. I was losing my mind without you. We belong together, Reggie. Can't you see that?"

As Martin answered the doorbell and escorted a police officer into the living room, Reggie released Caprice and said, "No, Pree. We don't. We never did. I belong with Bobbie."

Reggie backed away from her, walked over to me, and reached for my hand. As I took his hand and followed him out of the house, I could hear Caprice's voice behind us growing more and more distant as she screamed, "No! Reggie! No, I love you!"

***

The three of us, me, Reggie, and Martin, stood outside on Caprice's driveway and watched as the police escorted a handcuffed Caprice to a cruiser and helped her into the backseat.

I squeezed Reggie's hand as another officer approached us. "Mr. and Mrs. Darrough, I'm Sergeant Ambler."

Reggie took his extended hand. "Yes?"

"I just wanted you folks to know that we have put out a statewide APB on Francine Walker, and we *will* find her. We have your numbers. We will contact you when we have some concrete news for you."

"Thank you, Officer."

Reggie turned to Martin and shook his hand. "I don't know how we could ever repay you, Martin. Thank you."

Martin smiled. "No problem, man. Look, I'm gonna swing by my hotel and then head to Dallas to see if I can get some leads on Purifoy or Walker or whoever she is. I'll be in touch."

Before Martin could turn to leave, I said, "Wait. I'll go with you."

Martin glanced from me to Reggie. "Um…"

"Bobbie, no," Reggie said.

"No? You think you have the right to give me orders?"

"It wasn't an order. It's just not a good idea for you to go. Look, let's just go home. The police are on it and so is Martin. It makes no sense for you to go. Besides, your mother is probably on pins and needles right about now. We need to go home and get our heads right. As soon as Martin or the police get some information, we can head straight to Dallas."

I stood my ground. "I'm going."

Reggie groaned. "Then so am I."

I shrugged. "Fine."

He walked around and opened the passenger door. "Come on," he said.

"I'm riding with Martin," I retorted.

Reggie frowned. "What?!"

"After that little display in that house between you and *Pree*, I don't want to be near you."

"Bobbie, you know that was an act. I did what I had to do to get the information from her. You *know* I don't want her. She's crazy!"

"I don't care."

We stared each other down as Martin began to back away from us. "Look, I'll just be in my car..." Martin said softly.

"Martin, wait. Don't leave without me," I said, my eyes still on Reggie.

"Uh...yes, ma'am," Martin said as he slowly walked to his car.

"Bobbie, don't. Please don't do this, baby. Ride with me. Talk to me," Reggie pleaded.

I shook my head. "I can't. I just can't right now. I can't even look you in the face right now, Reggie."

"You need time?"

"Yes. If you're coming, fine. But I cannot ride with you right now."

"Okay." He leaned in and kissed my cheek. "I love you."

"I know you do."

I walked over to Martin's car and climbed inside. "Let's go," I said softly.

"Okay, Ms. Bobbie. You need anything?"

I nodded. "Yeah. A drink."

Thirty-One

"We're Ready"

Tomeka

Granny said that Aunt Bobbie Ann and Uncle Reggie had gone to Dallas to try to find the baby. I was worried about them and little Faith. I really hoped that they would find her and come back soon. I was worried about Granny, too. She wasn't hardly sleeping at all. I could hear her sometimes in the middle of the night moving around in her room since it was right next to me and Sharee's room. Sometimes I would hear her talking to God, praying for help. Sometimes I would hear her crying. But I hardly ever heard her sleeping.

I couldn't sleep, either. I was too worried about the baby and too excited about the idea of getting to see and talk to Abraham face-to-face. I was too happy about being able to hug him and see his smile and feel his touch. I was scared, too, though. I was a virgin. What if he wanted to do it right away? What if I wasn't good at doing it? I hadn't told him I was a virgin. I really wished I'd done it with Lavarius Smith when he asked me to. At least that way I'd have some experience. I was like a little kid. A virgin from the country who didn't even have a driver's license. What if he got tired of me?

But he said he loved me, and I believed him. So maybe he'd be patient with me. Maybe he wouldn't be too disappointed. Some guys even like being a girl's first. Maybe he would see it as an honor. But where would we do it? At his mother's house? Or maybe he'd get us a really nice hotel room with a heart-shaped bed—like a honeymoon suite or something, because this was going to be kind of like a honeymoon for us.

Maybe we'd drink champagne and he'd feed me strawberries dipped in chocolate. And there would be rose petals on the bed and then after we made love, we'd take a bubble bath in a big Jacuzzi. That would be nice.

I smiled and looked over at Sharee who was sleeping like she didn't have a care in the world. She was so young, and she knew nothing about love and life. I was so much more mature than her. And soon I would have to leave her so that I could be with Abraham. We hadn't really discussed what we were going to do once he got out of prison, but as much as we loved one another, I knew weren't going to be able to stay apart. We needed to be together and soon, we would be together forever.

***

Two days had passed and Aunt Bobbie Ann and Uncle Reggie were still in Dallas trying to find Faith, Granny was still worried, Sharee was still irritating, and I hadn't heard from Abraham. I tried to tell myself that it was still early. It had only been a few days since he'd heard he was going to be paroled. But I loved him, and I was just excited and impatient and ready to see him and be with him.

I kept my phone on me all the time in case he called so I wouldn't miss it. I even slept with it in my bra. I wouldn't miss that call for anything in the world.

I had just finished taking a shower and gotten dressed and was heading downstairs when I felt the phone vibrate in my pocket. I hurried down the stairs and through the living room to the backyard as fast as I could. I didn't stop running until I had reached the rear of the pool house.

I hit the button to accept the call and was out of breath as I said, "Hello?!"

"Angel, it's me," Abraham sang into the phone.

"Oh, Abraham! You're…you're out?"

"Yes, and I wanna see you, baby. I wanna see you *right now*."

"Okay, um, I gotta eat breakfast first, and then I'll see if I can sneak out to the community park here. I'ma need time to call the guard shack and let them know to let you in."

"Guard shack? Dang, your auntie rich, huh?"

"Something like that," I said and then gave him the address.

"How much time you need?"

"About an hour should be good. I can't wait, Abraham!"

"Me either, angel. Adios."

I smiled. "Adios."

Thirty-Two

"One More Shot"

Bobbie

I held the bottle to my lips and threw my head back, relishing every drop of liquor that slid down my throat. I swallowed the last drop, shook my head, and set the bottle on the floor next to the bed. I opened my eyes to see Martin staring at me from his seat at the table. I noticed the still-full bottle of liquor that sat in front of him.

"You still over there nursing that bottle?" I slurred.

He sighed and nodded his head. "Yeah."

I stumbled to my feet and slowly made my way across the hotel room to him. I reached for the bottle, but he moved it before I could get my hands on it.

"What are you doing, Ms. Bobbie?" he asked.

"If you ain't gon' drink it, I will."

He looked me in the eye. "No, I think you've had enough."

I stared down at him, confused by his words and his actions. The three days we'd spent in that hotel, he'd been my nightly, or actually, early morning drinking buddy, and now he was the voice of sobriety? I just didn't get it.

"Give me the bottle, Martin," I demanded.

"No."

I could feel anger swelling inside of me. I needed that drink. I needed to numb the emotions that threatened to destroy what was left of my sanity. I *needed* it. "*Why?*"

"Because you're better than this."

I rolled my eyes. "No, I'm not."

He stood to face me and rested a hand on my shoulder. "Your husband is down the hall worried sick about you and your baby. He wants nothing more than to love you and comfort you." He picked up the bottle. "You don't need this. You need *him*."

I smiled up at him and rested my hand on his chest. "Maybe I need you. You give me that bottle and I'll show you some things."

"I'ma pretend I didn't hear that because I know it's just the liquor talking."

I cocked my head to the side. "You don't want me?"

"Hell yeah I do," he said softly. "You know I do, but I can't."

"Why?"

"I can't because if I really wanted to, I could make you love me. I could take you away from your husband and make no mistake, I would treat you real good for a while. But I'm not a good man, Ms. Bobbie. Your husband is a good man, and right now he's sitting in his room alone. No baby. No wife. And he doesn't deserve that."

He backed away from me, took the bottle to the bathroom, and poured its contents down the sink.

"Why the hell you do that?!"

"Because the last thing you need to be when we find your little girl is drunk! You need to sober the hell up and get your mind right, baby."

I walked over to the bed, sat down, and lowered my head. "You still think we'll find her?" I looked up at him. "Because I don't."

Martin walked over to me and kneeled in front of me, placing his hands on my knees. "I got good sources here in Dallas. I got a couple of friends that owe me favors, and they both work for the police force. They got good leads on the couple that might have bought the baby. I'ma find your baby, Ms. Bobbie. That's not a question in my mind. The only question I have is will you be able to take care of her when I find her? Or will you be too drunk to even hold her?"

I sat there silently and stared at him. He finally stood and walked back over to his seat at the table. After a few quiet moments between us I said, "Why do you drink?"

He looked over at me. "What?"

"I know why I drink. Why do you drink? What are you trying to fix with alcohol?"

Martin dropped his eyes. "Damn, I wish I hadn't thrown out that booze," he muttered.

I walked into the bathroom, plugged in the coffeemaker, and began to fill the small coffee pot with water.

"What you doing, sexy?" he asked softly.

"I'ma make us both some coffee and we're going to sober up and you're going to tell me why you drink."

As I placed the prepackaged filter and coffee grounds into the coffeemaker, Martin said, "I drink because I killed my wife."

***

I sipped my coffee and listened intently as Martin spoke just above a whisper.

"I met my wife in high school. We grew up together."

I smiled. "That's how it was with Reggie and me."

He gave me a small smile and continued. "Uh, we got married right out of high school and uh, I enlisted in the service and after basic training, got stationed in Guam. She didn't mind moving there. She had a bad family life and so did I, so we were glad just to have each other.

"Anyway, we moved around a lot as I climbed the ranks, until we finally moved to Washington where I was promoted again and asked to work on a special task force for the president. I worked long hours, traveled a lot, was barely ever home. My wife complained all the time about being lonely and it didn't help that as hard as we tried, we couldn't have any kids and she wanted kids more than anything in the world. She was depressed, and I wasn't around enough to notice it. "

He sighed and shook his head. "The last trip I took before her death, I did as I usually did. I called her every night before I went to bed and told her I loved her and couldn't wait to come back home to her. She told me she loved me—that she'd always love me, and then she hung up. I tried to call her back several times because she just didn't sound right to me. I…uh…" his voice began to break.

I reached over and grasped both of his hands. "It's okay, Martin," I whispered.

He shook his head. "No it's not! I fell asleep, Bobbie. I was so damn tired from working my important job that I fell asleep! When I woke up the next morning, I called and called and she wouldn't answer the phone. *She wouldn't answer…*" And then Martin, who, to me, was synonymous with cool and calm, began to sob. I stood and wrapped my arms around him and rubbed his back and felt my own tears begin to form.

"I…I took the first plane back home and when I walked through the door to my house, I felt a chill in the air. It was like all of the life had been sucked out of that place. I walked into our bedroom and there she was lying in the bed—cold. She was gone. She's taken an overdose of some sleeping pills I didn't even know she had. Can't you see? I killed her and, sometimes, the alcohol dulls the pain just a little bit, but it never goes away. I carry my guilt with me everywhere I go."

I continued to hold him. "Is that when you started drinking?"

He sniffled. "Yeah. I drank myself out of the military. I drank myself homeless. Then one day, an old friend saw me on the street. One of my old military buddies I'd known since basic training. He took me into his home. He'd become a minister and he and his family helped me. I was sober for ten years after that."

"What made you fall off the wagon?"

He shrugged. "I just got tired of trying, I guess. I got tired of the work it takes to stay sober."

I held his face in my hands. "What if I make you a deal? If you stay sober, so will I. We can be each other's accountability partner."

He chuckled lightly. "You still tryna get in my pants, sexy?"

I felt my face heat up. "No, and I'm sorry about that. Liquor makes me do some stupid stuff. I never would've approached you like that if I wasn't half-way drunk. I'm upset with Reggie but I love him with all my heart."

"Then why are you in my room at 4:00 A.M. instead of his?"

I sighed. "I don't know."

"Look, as much as I love your company, you need to leave and go make things right with him. He's a good guy."

"Too good for me. Even when he messes up, he's better than me."

"Maybe so, Ms. Bobbie. But he loves you, and he needs you right now. You need each other."

I nodded. "I know. Did you mean what you said earlier? You really believe you'll find Faith?"

He smiled. "I *know* it."

"Okay." I released him, patted his back, and walked towards the door.

"Where you going?"

"To talk to Reggie. You never answered my question, Martin."

He stared at me then walked over to me and kissed my cheek. "Yes. I'll be your accountability partner."

I smiled up at him. "Good. Talk to you later."

He nodded. "Yeah."

As the door softly closed behind me, I walked down the hall and knocked on Reggie's door.

Thirty-Three

"Darling Baby"

Tomeka

I sat on a bench in the park, waiting for Abraham to arrive. I had butterflies in my stomach as I stared at the street. I wondered what kind of car he'd be in and what he would be wearing. I rubbed my hand over my little pleated skirt and smoothed the front of my white shirt. I called this outfit my "school girl" outfit. The skirt showed off my legs, and the shirt showed off my breasts. I dug in my purse and pulled out my cherry-flavored lip gloss, slid it across my lips, and then smacked them together. I checked my hair in the small mirror I kept in my purse and checked my watch for the hundredth time.

He was late. Maybe he wasn't coming. I checked the screen of my cell phone. Wouldn't he call if he wasn't coming? Maybe something happened to him. Was he in a wreck? Was he hurt? Oh, no, what if they changed their minds and put him back in jail? What if—

I jumped up from the bench when I saw the car stop on the side of the street. Could it be—was it *him*?

I held my breath and stood there staring at the car. No one got out. They just sat there. The windows were too darkly tinted for me to see inside. So I just stood there and waited and hoped it was him. When the door finally opened and Abraham climbed out, I almost fainted. I smiled and before I even knew what I was doing, I took off running towards him. When I made it to the car, he grabbed me and hugged me so tightly that I thought he'd crush me, but it still felt good to finally be in his arms.

We hugged for a long time. I don't think either of us could believe that this moment was really happening. After months of letters and phone calls, we were finally together, touching each other and seeing each other and smelling each other. When Abraham let me go, his hands shook as he moved them to my face and leaned in close.

"I'm so glad I can finally do this," he whispered.

Then he kissed me really softly—like he was afraid my lips would break if he pressed too hard against them. Our lips parted, and Abraham smiled at me. I smiled back at him, and then his expression changed. He got this serious look on his face, and he leaned in again. This time, he held me around my waist and kissed me *for real*. Like in the movies—my first real kiss. I had never been kissed like that and no one had ever held me so closely. And nothing in my life had ever felt so good. I felt like I was going to lose my mind if he didn't stop kissing me and when he stopped, I felt like I would lose my mind if he didn't kiss me again.

He ended the kiss and backed away from me, and I could tell he was trying to catch his breath. And then a feeling came over me. I needed to kiss him again. *I really did.* So I reached for him and pulled him back to me and kissed him. Another *real* kiss. He grabbed me around the waist again and pulled me even closer to him—so close that I could feel his chest rise and fall as he breathed. He felt so strong and warm, and I could've died right then and there and I would've been okay with it. Kissing Abraham Rios was like a dream come true—a perfect fantasy.

We held each other for a long time, him kissing me and me kissing him. His hands on my hips or my back or my face. My arms around his neck. I wished that moment could go on forever.

Abraham finally let me go and looked into my eyes and said, "Can you go somewhere with me?"

"Yeah."

I didn't even think about my answer or the consequences of my leaving with Abraham. Granny didn't even know I'd left the house. When she found out she'd be worried, but I didn't think about that either. I didn't think about any of that because I didn't care about anything at that moment except for how I felt. I felt like I was going to explode with love for Abraham. And I never wanted to be away from him again.

He smiled and kissed me softly. "Good. I won't keep you out long. I just need to be with you."

I nodded. "Me, too."

I climbed into the passenger seat of the car, a Chevy Impala he bought and put in his mama's name before he got sent to prison. And I closed my eyes and rested my head on the back of the seat as Abraham drove us out of my aunt's gated neighborhood.

Thirty-Four

"Why I Sing The Blues"

Bobbie

Reggie answered the door wearing a t-shirt and a pair of jeans, stubble shadowing his face. His face bore the expression of a man who'd been beaten down but was still trying to hold on.

"You're up early," I said softly.

"I haven't been to sleep," he answered. "I knocked on your door a little earlier. You weren't there."

I sighed. "I know. I was drinking with Martin."

His facial expression changed. His eyes darted towards Martin's door as he clenched his fists. "Why would he be drinking with you?" he asked though his teeth.

I placed a hand on his chest. "Can I come in? I'll explain."

He stood there, his eyes drifting from me to Martin's door and back to me.

I reached up and caressed his rough cheek. "Please let me in."

He nodded hesitantly and then backed out of the doorway.

I sat on his undisturbed bed as he turned the TV off and sat down beside me. I looked over at him and rested my hand over his as tears began to fill my eyes. "I'm sorry, Reggie," I whispered. "I…I've been drinking every night since we've been in Dallas."

"With Martin?" he asked quietly.

"Yes."

"Why would he do that? What is he trying to get from you?" he said, his voice strained.

I shook my head. "No, baby, he's not like that. He's been through a lot and he's…he's an alcoholic, too. I guess we just have this common bond between us. He understands me."

"And you think I don't?"

I looked him in the eye. "I *know* you do, Reggie. But I was hurt about you and Caprice. I'm still hurt and I want my baby back and I just feel like there's no hope. I feel like giving up…on everything."

He frowned and cupped my face in his hands. "You *can't* give up. I'm sorry. I'm sincerely sorry for the part I played in our baby's disappearance. I'm sorry for what I did with Caprice and for keeping it from you. I'm sorry that I haven't been able to find Faith. I'm sorry for failing you, Bobbie. But please don't give up on me or our marriage. Please don't give up hope of finding our daughter."

I watched as a single tear trailed down his face. I gently wiped it away. "Reggie, I don't want to give up, but I don't know what else to do. I don't know how to cope with all of this. The only thing I know how to do is drink. That's how I deal with things. I want to drink right now so badly." I collapsed against him, my sobs shaking both of our bodies.

"Shh, baby. It's okay. I love you. I love you and Faith so much," he whispered soothingly. Here he was, just as hurt as I was and he hadn't fallen apart and gone down some self-destructive path. At least not this time.

"How do you do it? How do you cope with things without falling apart?" I asked.

He released me and held my face in his hands as he wiped my tears with his thumbs. "I pray, baby. I get down on my knees or I lie on my face and I talk to God. I pray sometimes until I can't think of anything else to say, and then I just close my eyes and listen and try to feel God's arms around me. I pray because that's all I know to do. The only thing that I've got is my faith, Bobbie. That's how I cope. I trust God and you know what, He's never—not once—let me down. *Never.* No matter how bad things seem, I know He's got my back. He's got yours, too, baby.

"You've just got to learn how to exercise your faith. What's in those bottles can never heal you or help you. I can be here for you, but I can't save you, either. Only Jesus can do that. Don't you know that?"

I nodded. "I do know that, but sometimes it's just so hard to see it and to believe it. Especially when everything is falling apart."

Reggie shook his head. "No, baby. Trusting God is easy. It's the easiest thing in the world to do once you realize He's always been there with you, taking care of you. When has He ever failed you?"

I closed my eyes as warm tears wet my cheeks. "Never."

"Then trust Him, baby. Trust that whatever happens, He's got your back."

"I do," I said softly.

We sat there in silence until I spoke again. "Reggie, me and Martin didn't do anything but drink together, but—"

"It doesn't matter, Bobbie."

"No, I need to tell you. I almost—"

Reggie kissed me lightly on the lips. "It doesn't matter. You were hurt. I hurt you, and I'm sorry. Whatever did or didn't happen doesn't matter."

I wrapped my arms around him and gripped him tightly. "Oh, Reggie…"

There was a knock at Reggie's door. He kissed my forehead and left the bed to answer it. He checked the peep hole then turned and looked at me as he opened the door. Martin walked in and before either Reggie or I could say a word, he said, "I just got a call from my friend at the Dallas PD. They found your baby."

Thirty-Five

"Lovin' My Baby"

Tomeka

My hands shook as I followed Abraham through the lobby to the elevator. It was a nice hotel. The nicest I'd ever been in. It was beautiful, and I was sure our room would be really nice, but that didn't change the fact that I was a virgin or that Abraham didn't know it.

I followed him onto the elevator and he took my hand in his and squeezed it. I gave him a quick little smile then looked down at my feet. As the elevator began to move, he leaned over and whispered in my ear.

"You sure you want to do this?" he asked then kissed my cheek.

My heart began to race again. I made sure to steady my voice before I spoke. "Yes."

He smiled. "Good."

The elevator stopped at the fourth floor. With my hand in his, I trailed Abraham down a hallway with carpet so soft, it felt like my feet sunk into every step. He unlocked the door with a card, and we walked inside. There was no heart-shaped bed and no roses. There wasn't any champagne chilling for us, and I didn't see any chocolate-covered strawberries. But the room was really nice, and the bed was huge with white sheets and a white comforter. The window gave us a nice view of downtown Houston.

Abraham closed the door behind us, and I just stood there in the middle of the floor not sure what I should do. When he turned around, he looked at me and smiled. "You look scared, angel. Are you scared?"

I frowned a little, fought back tears, and shook my head.

He walked over to me and rubbed the side of my face gently with his hand. "Are you a virgin, Meka?"

I looked from Abraham's face to the wall and shook my head again.

He reached around and pulled the rubber band from my hair. Then he dug his fingers into my hair and kissed me again. I closed my eyes and kissed him back and suddenly, I forgot about being nervous or worrying about impressing him. I remembered that I loved him, and I wanted to be with him more than anything else in the world. I remembered that we belonged together. He began to move forward, gently pushing me backwards at the same time until I felt the bed behind me. We lay down together and in that pretty hotel room, on those white sheets, underneath the white covers, I stopped being a little girl. I became a woman.

Thirty-Six

"Blues For My Baby"

Bobbie

I sat on the passenger's side of Reggie's car and stared at the Tudor-style home. It was a nice house with nice cars in the driveway. The couple definitely had money, probably more than enough money to buy a baby, *my baby*. But was that really my baby inside of that house? What if this was all a mistake? What if they hadn't found Faith? How was I going to deal with the disappointment?

I turned and looked at Martin who sat in the backseat. "Did your friend tell you what their names were?"

He shook his head. "No. He didn't give me any details other than the address and the fact that they've only been married a year or so."

"I see. Thank you."

I turned my attention back to the house as I reached over and grasped Reggie's hand. He never took his eyes off of that house.

It boggled my mind that someone would actually buy a child. It just seemed like a nightmare to think that if it weren't for Martin, we might've had to go on with our lives not knowing that our little girl was growing up just a drive down the highway away from us. The police still hadn't even called to notify us of the possibility of this couple having Faith. If it weren't for Martin's friend, we'd still be in the dark.

My heart began to thump in my chest as I watched an officer escort a thin woman out of the house. She kept her head down, making it impossible for me to see her face. Her shoulders shook as if she was crying. I looked over at Reggie whose eyes were glued to the woman. After they'd placed her in the police cruiser, Reggie stared at it, one hand gripping mine, the other tightening and loosening its grip on the steering wheel.

"Baby, you okay?" I asked.

He shook his head, his eyes still fixed on the police car. "No."

Then his face changed and with his eyes still on the house he said, "Bobbie."

I frowned as I shifted my eyes from my husband's face to the scene outside the house. There, being escorted to a cruiser with a look of sheer panic on his face was Clyde Morgan, my ex-husband. Or at least it looked like him. But surely it wasn't. That would just be too bizarre.

Without even fully realizing what I was doing, I opened the door, forgetting that I wasn't even supposed to be there, that I wasn't supposed to know that Faith might be in that house. I climbed out of the car, ignoring Martin's urges for me to stop and snatching away from Reggie's grip on my arm. I began to walk across the street, towards the house and my ex-husband and his wife. I could hear rapid footsteps behind me. I could hear Reggie calling my name. But I had to see if it was really him. I had to know why.

"Clyde?!" I yelled as the officer helped Clyde into the backseat.

Both Clyde and the officer stopped and looked in my direction. "Bobbie? What you doing here?"

"The baby. The one you *bought*? It's mine."

"What the hell? Now, wait just a minute. That woman told me that baby's mama was some young girl from Galveston. That can't be your baby!"

"Get inside, sir," the officer demanded. "Ma'am, please step away from the vehicle."

"No, I'm gonna find out why my ex-husband *bought* my child!"

"Bobbie, I swear I didn't know that was your baby. I would never do anything like that to you. You know how I feel about you, little girl. Phaea can't have kids and I was just tryna make her happy. I—" The officer shoved Clyde into the car and shut the door on him mid-sentence.

"I'm sorry, Bobbie," Clyde mouthed through the window.

"Sorry? Why the hell would you buy a baby? Why didn't you just adopt?!" I screamed.

I felt Reggie tug on my arm as I was just about to light into the officer for interrupting our conversation. "Baby…" he said softly, his voice breaking with every syllable.

I turned around, my heart galloping, and focused my eyes on the police officer who was holding a precious little baby girl. She was beautiful, but she wasn't mine. I collapsed against Reggie in inconsolable tears.

Thirty-Seven

"Forever"

Tomeka

I lay in bed next to Abraham with my eyes closed. What we did felt good and bad at the same time. I was confused about it. Actually, I didn't know how I was supposed to feel. But I knew I still loved him and if he wanted to do it again, I probably would.

He put his arm around my waist and pulled me closer to him. "Why you lie about being a virgin?" he asked as he slid his hand up and down my back.

I shrugged. "I don't know. I guess I thought you wouldn't want to be with me if you knew."

"I'ma always want to be with you, Meka. I love you. Don't you know that?"

"Yes."

"You ain't never got to lie to me about nothing, baby. And besides, being a virgin ain't nothing to be ashamed of. I'm glad you saved yourself for me. This means we're bonded forever."

I looked up at his face. "It does?"

"Yeah. Did you…did you like it?"

I dropped my eyes. "I don't know. It kinda hurt."

He rubbed his hand across my hair and kissed my forehead. "I'm sorry. But the more you do it, the better it is."

"Really?"

"Yeah."

I laid there against him and thought for a moment. Then I said, "Can we do it again?"

"You sure you want to?"

"Yeah, I'm sure."

Abraham scooted down in the bed to face me and kissed me softly and this time he was very gentle with me. And he was right, it was much better.

***

I stood in the bathroom of our hotel room and stared into the mirror trying to see if I looked different, because I sure felt different. I felt sad and happy all at the same time. Sad because I knew it was wrong to do what we did. Happy because I was with Abraham. I sighed as I combed my hair and put it into a ponytail. I put on a fresh coat of lip gloss and then stepped out of the bathroom and back into the room where Abraham sat on the bed in his starched khakis and white shirt and stared at me.

"You ready to go?" he asked.

I shrugged my shoulders. "Not really."

"Come here."

I walked over to him and stood right in front of him. He wrapped his arms around me. "You okay? Did I hurt you again?"

"No, I'm fine. I...can we just stay here for a little while longer?"

He smiled up at me. "We can do whatever you want, angel. You hungry?"

I smiled. "Yeah, I am."

"How about we get some room service, and then I'll take you back. Okay?"

"Okay."

We ate and then we climbed back into the bed. I ended up falling asleep. It was after dark before I woke up. And I knew I was in trouble.

Thirty-Eight

"It's My Own Fault Baby"

Bobbie

I sat in the car across the street from Clyde's house and stared at his perfectly manicured lawn. It still wasn't over. My little girl was still missing, and my heart was still broken. I looked over at Reggie who looked even more defeated than I felt. I wasn't sure how much more he could take. I wasn't sure how far away my breaking point was, either.

We were sitting in the back seat waiting for Martin to finish his phone call, and then he was to drive us back to the hotel where we would resume the wait—the agonizing, excruciatingly painful wait for news about our daughter. I was so tired of waiting. Hell, I was just tired of being tired. And though it was the last thing I needed, I wanted a drink worse than anything else in the world. Anything, that is, except for my baby. I would've walked through fire to find her.

I reached over and grasped Reggie's hand. He looked over at me, his eyes puffy, and the smooth brown skin of his cheeks tear-streaked.

"I'm sorry, baby," he said softly. "I failed. If you wanna leave me, I understand. I wouldn't blame you. I know this is all my fault."

I closed my eyes and shook my head. "I don't want to leave you,

Reggie. I just want my little girl back. That's all I want."

He dropped his head as tears streamed down his face. "I do, too."

I reached over and pulled him close to me. I held him tightly and tried to comfort him while at the same time trying to comfort myself. We were still locked in each other's arms when Martin climbed into the driver's seat of the car.

"Um, excuse me," he said softly.

I released Reggie and wiped my wet face. "Yes?" I replied.

Martin sighed. "Look, I have another lead. Someone left a baby at one of the local hospitals. It's a black female who looks to be around the same age as your baby. I'm gonna go check it out. I know you two have been through a lot and you must be drained. I can drop you off at the hotel and then head over to the hospital myself to check it out."

"But how will you know if it's her? Don't we need to identify her?" Reggie asked.

"I can take a picture with my phone and send it to you," Martin suggested.

Reggie looked at me and shook his head. "No, we'll go with you."

Martin nodded. "Okay."

***

Reggie and I followed Martin through the huge hospital to the pediatric ward, hands tightly clasped, hearts hopeful and cautious at the same time. With every step I took, I prayed to God that this was our child and that the nightmare would finally be over.

When we arrived, a social worker met us and explained to us that the baby had been left in a carrier in the ER waiting area a couple of days earlier. There was no note, just a little African American baby girl left all alone on the floor next to a chair. No one saw who left her, and it was only after she began crying that someone noticed she was alone. They had run a story on the local news stations about her, but hadn't received any viable information about the baby's parents. They had run tests and she was perfectly healthy. If she wasn't Faith, she would be sent to foster care later that day.

If she was Faith, I wondered why Mrs. Purifoy had left her there like that. Had the deal to sell her fallen through?

"You can go in to see her whenever you're ready," the social worker said.

Reggie looked down at me and squeezed my hand. "Ready, baby?"

I nodded. "As long as we're together, I'm ready for anything."

Martin opened the door to room 14P, and lying there in a crib and wearing a little hospital gown, was the love of my life—my little girl.

Thirty-Nine

"Blues Is Here To Stay"

Bobbie

After dealing with the police and all of their questions and answers and unanswered questions, we were able to leave Dallas with our daughter and head back home around seven that evening. I was glad because I really didn't want to spend another night in that hotel. I was glad the ordeal was over. So glad that I wasn't that upset about the police letting Francine Walker or Vera Purifoy or whoever she was slip through their fingers. But I prayed that they'd catch her and that I never saw her on the streets, because I couldn't be responsible for what I'd do to her.

They still had Clyde and Phaea and Caprice in custody and as far as I was concerned, they could all form a singing trio in hell. It didn't matter to me whose baby Clyde bought. The fact remained that the sick fool purchased *someone's* baby, and that was just about the lowest thing a human could do.

As I sat in the backseat, singing one of my daddy's favorite old blues songs and staring at my little girl, I thought my heart would burst with love for her. It was beyond me how I ever saw her as a burden or how I ever resented caring for her. When she was missing, I'd longed to change her diapers and feel her warm body next to mine as she nursed. As I sat there watching her, I vowed to never let her out of my sight again. Even if I had to take her into the studio with me and let her cry in the background or wheel her onstage in a stroller, she was never leaving me again. I was even willing to give up my career if I had to. She was just that important. She was even more important than that.

I reached over and rubbed her hair as she slept soundly. I closed my eyes and thanked God in my mind over and over again. I leaned my head back against the seat and rested my hand on her tiny leg.

"Everything okay back there?" Reggie asked.

I opened my eyes and met his in the rearview mirror. "Everything is perfect."

Reggie smiled. "It sure is. I got my two girls with me and the best cook on Earth is at my house right now probably whipping up a celebration dinner for us. And to top it all off, the best singer in the world is in my backseat, blessing me with her voice. God is good, baby."

"He sure is. I think I'll call Mama and see what she cooked. I didn't get to talk to her long when I called to tell her about Faith earlier. The police were all in my face with their questions. But I could tell she was excited."

"Yeah, call and see what we got to look forward to."

I dialed the number to my house and looked back over at my baby. I think a part of me still couldn't believe she was back with us. I needed to keep my eyes on her to be sure she was real.

"Hello?" Mama answered, sounding strained.

"Hey, Mama. I just wanted to let you know we're on our way home. You okay?"

Ignoring my question, she said, "Is dat detective man wit' y'all?"

I glanced at Reggie. "Well, no, he's headed back to his hotel. I invited him to dinner but he declined. Why?"

"You got his number?"

"Yes. Mama, what is going on?"

"Tomeka gone."

"What? Tomeka is gone *where*?"

"I don't know. I didn't even know she was gone 'til a little while ago. I ain't seent her since dis mornin', but I thought she was down in da basement or somethin'. Sharee say she been gone all day."

"Well, where could she possibly be?"

"I don't know, Bobbie Ann! Dat's why you need to call dat Martin." Mama was beginning to sound frantic.

"Okay, I'll have him meet us at the house. Mama, you need to go ahead and call the police."

"Okay. Y'all hurry up and get here."

"Yes, ma'am. I think we're about halfway there." I hung up and searched my phone for Martin's number.

"What's going on, Bobbie?" Reggie asked.

"Tomeka is missing."

***

It was after 10:00 P.M. by the time we made it home. Martin pulled into the driveway right behind us and we all walked in together. We found Mama sitting in the living room wringing her hands. Sharee was sitting next to her looking like she was near tears.

I handed Faith to Reggie and rushed to my mother's side. I wrapped my arm around her shoulder. "Did you call the police, Mama?" I asked softly.

"Yeah. They done been here and gone. I gave 'em a picture. They gon' try to find her but they say it's gone be hard since I don't have no clue what time she leff' or where she was goin'."

Out of the corner of my eye I could see Martin shaking his head. "Mrs. Brooks, does Tomeka have any friends here in town? Anyone that could've picked her up?" he asked.

"She got a pen pal name Claudia. I already told da police dat."

"Claudia lives here in Houston?" I asked.

Mama nodded.

"Pen pal? Do you know if she brought any of the letters here with her?" Martin said.

"Naw, like I told them police. She guard them letters like they Fort Knox. Won't let nobody near 'em."

"I…I know where one is," Sharee said quietly.

All eyes were on Sharee now. "You do? Why you ain't say dat when da police was here?" Mama asked.

She shrugged. "Cause you told me not to say nothing."

"Where is it Sharee?" I asked.

"I stole one of 'em. She was always hiding them and stuff, and I wanted to know what they was talking about that was so secret." She pulled the envelope from the back pocket of her jeans and handed it to Mama.

Mama handed it to me. "My nerves is too bad ta' read it."

I handed it to Martin who pulled out his phone and began to plug the address into his GPS. "It's across town in a pretty rough area. Be best to call first," he said. He stared at the envelope for a second. "Claudia Rios. Let me see if I can get my assistant to find a number for her. I'll be right back." He handed the envelope back to me and stepped out into the foyer to make his phone call.

I held the envelope in my hand and then opened it and pulled out the letter. My eyes widened as I read the words before me and when I saw the name signed at the bottom, I looked at Sharee and said, "Who is Abraham?"

Sharee shook her head. "I don't know. She wouldn't tell me. She never tells me anything anymore." She wiped a tear from her cheek. "But I did hear her praying that he would get out."

"Get out? Get out of what?" Mama asked.

I leaned back against the couch and held my hand over my mouth. He was an inmate. That's why she always acted so strange when we went to visit Junior. This inmate was the boy she "liked".

"He's in prison," I said softly.

Mama looked at me like I had lost my mind. "What?!" she shrieked. "How she meet a inmate?"

I shrugged and glanced over at Reggie whose face read a mixture of worry and anger. "I don't know, Mama. I guess she got in contact with him somehow during our visits to see Junior."

Mama stood and began to pace the floor. "Lawd, Jesus. Lawd, Jesus…"

Martin walked back into the room. "Okay, she couldn't find a number for a Claudia Rios, but there was one for an Estelita Rios at the same address. I'm going to call over there now and see if they know Tomeka."

"Um… she has a phone," Sharee said barely above a whisper.

"Who? Claudia?" I asked.

She shook her head. "No, Tomeka."

Mama stopped in her tracks. "Whatchu say, Sharee?"

"Tomeka's got a phone."

Mama frowned. "Since when?"

"I don't know. A few weeks, I guess. I heard her talking on it late one night when she thought I was sleep."

"Where she git it?" Mama asked the question before I could.

"I don't know."

"Sharee, why didn'tchu tell me?" Mama asked.

"I guess I didn't want Meka to get mad at me for telling. She's always calling me a tattletale and stuff."

"Do you know the number, Sharee?" Martin asked.

Sharee nodded. "Yeah. I wrote it down. Let me go get it."

Sharee hurried from the room, and silence fell over all of us. I was sure that Mama and Reggie and I had coordinated thoughts at that moment, wondering how none of us had noticed she had a cell phone and was corresponding with an inmate. How had we let Tomeka slip through our fingers like this?

Sharee quickly returned with Tomeka's number, but before anyone even had time to dial it, there was a knock at the front door. Reggie handed Faith to me and went to answer it. When he returned, Tomeka was with him. And standing behind her, a young Hispanic man.

Forty

"Guess Who"

Tomeka

I stood there, my legs weak and my hands shaking and everyone, including Mr. Martin, staring at me and Abraham, and I knew his idea to come into the house and meet everyone was a really bad one.

Granny walked over to me and said, "Girl, where is you been?! Yo' cousin is back home safe and sound and we 'spose ta be celebratin', but instead, we all sittin' 'round here worried 'bout yo' little narrow behind! And who is dis? Da inmate you been writin'?"

I gasped. How did she know I'd been writing Abraham or that he was an inmate? Then I looked over at Sharee who was looking all sneaky and crazy, and I knew she'd spilled the beans. She'd snuck around and found out about Abraham and told the world.

"Don't look at Sharee. Look at me!" Granny shouted. "Who dis man you wit'?!"

"Ms. Mae, he says his name is Abraham Rios. Just say the word and I'll take care of him," Uncle Reggie said. And from the look on his face and his balled-up fists, I was sure his definition of taking care of Abraham was different from mine.

"This…this is Abraham, Granny," I repeated.

"How old is you, Abraham?" Granny asked.

"Twenty-two, ma'am."

"Twenty-two!" Aunt Bobbie Ann yelled. "Do you know how old Tomeka is?"

"Yes, ma'am. It's not what you think. We're just friends."

Aunt Bobbie Ann shoved a letter in Abraham's face. "This sounds like more than friendship to me!"

Abraham took the letter and dropped his head a little. "Yes, ma'am. I do care about Tomeka, but I know she's too young to be in a relationship with me."

"Then what the hell are you doing with her?" Aunt Bobbie Ann asked.

"We were…we were just talking. Tomeka's letters really helped me when I was on the inside. I came to depend on them."

"Did you touch her?" said Aunt Bobbie Ann.

"No!" I shouted.

Granny walked over to us and stood right in front of Abraham. "Young man, I'm tellin' you right now. I don't ever wanna hear 'bout you sniffin' 'round my granddaughter again. If you do, I'm callin' da police first chance I get. Now, you betta' go on."

Abraham stood frozen. "Ma'am, can I ask you something?"

"Ms. Mae? You want me to escort him out?" Uncle Reggie asked.

"Naw, Reggie. Dat's okay," Granny said. "Go on and ask it, young man."

"Is there any way possible that I can stay in contact with Tomeka? If not face-to-face, then maybe we can keep writing each other. It would mean a lot to both of us."

Uncle Reggie stepped forward. "I can answer that. No, you can't. She is a child, and you had no business contacting her in the first place. Let me show you the way out."

Abraham looked at me and gave me a little smile before following Uncle Reggie to the front door. I turned and looked from Aunt Bobbie Ann to Granny. "Please, Granny. Please don't do this. I…I love him!"

Granny shook her head. "You don't even know what love is, Meka. You jus' a baby."

I shook my head as I began to cry. I ran from the living room to the window next to the front door. I moved the curtains to the side and pressed my face against the window as I watched Abraham get into his car and back out of the driveway. I fell to my knees and began to sob loudly. It felt like my heart had been shot full of holes. I felt like I was actually dying inside.

Aunt Bobbie Ann came into the foyer and kneeled beside me. "Meka, I know you think you're in love, but you'll get over this. It'll just take some time."

I looked at her. "You said you fell in love with Uncle Reggie when you were a teenager. Did you get over him?"

Her eyes widened. "Well, Meka, that's different."

"Why? Because Abraham's older than me or because he's Mexican or because he was in prison? I don't care about that stuff! He's a good person and I love him, Aunt Bobbie Ann. I love him, and I can't live without him!"

She put her hand on my shoulder, and I shook it loose. I jumped to my feet and ran from the house and stood in the driveway and cried.

"Meka! Meka, come back inside!" Aunt Bobbie Ann shouted.

Then I heard Uncle Reggie's voice. He was standing right beside me. "Meka, I know it hurts, but it's gonna be okay. You gotta come inside and talk to your granny. You really worried her when you disappeared like that."

I wiped my cheeks. "I wasn't trying to worry anyone, Uncle Reggie. We just wanted to be together."

"Well, Meka, when you make decisions to do things like that, you gotta deal with the consequences, You've gotta come inside and face your granny, okay? Anything any of us say or do is out of love. We love you, and we're worried about you. We don't want anything to happen to you."

"I know that. But Abraham would never hurt me. He could've dropped me off at the gate and kept going, but he wanted to make sure I made it to the house safely, and he wanted to meet my family. He's a good person, Uncle Reggie."

Uncle Reggie nodded. "You know, Meka, I believe he *is* a good person, and I believe you love him. But that doesn't change the fact that you're underage, and he did not have your granny's permission to pick you up. You were wrong. *Both* of you were wrong."

I dropped my head. I knew he was right, but when a person is in love, they do crazy things sometimes, don't they? "I'm sorry."

"Don't apologize to me. Come on inside and apologize to your granny, okay?"

I sighed. "Okay."

Uncle Reggie wrapped his arm around my shoulder and led me back into the house.

"Uncle Reggie, I'm glad Faith is back home," I said.

"So am I."

Forty-One

"Stay Around A Little Longer"

Bobbie

I walked Martin to his car while Tomeka underwent Mama's interrogation. "Thank you so much," I said once we reached his rented Cadillac.

"No problem. Glad to help. Y'all take care of that little girl. Don't let her out of your sight," he said as he unlocked the car door. "Don't let *either* of them out of your sight—her or your niece."

"Yeah, well, Faith we can handle. We have new locks on all of the doors and we changed the security codes. We'll all be safe and sound in there. Now my niece, that's a much taller order. She really thinks she's in love with this man. I hope to God she was telling the truth. I hope she didn't do anything with him."

"Yeah, me, too. One thing I can tell you: I fell in love when I was young, and I ended up marrying the girl. If she feels the same way I did, she's not going to just forget about him."

I nodded. "I know."

He smiled down at me. "Another place and time, and you would be

Mrs. Miller."

I returned his smile. "I bet I would. You take care, and be careful."

"I'm just heading home. As they say in the movies, my work here is done."

"I feel like I've known you forever and yet, I have no idea where 'home' is."

"Memphis, baby. Home of the blues, the birthplace of rock and roll, and where I hang my hat. You got my number. Call me if you need me."

I reached up and hugged him. "I will. Don't forget we're buddies, now. I'ma call you, and I expect you to call me. Anytime, Martin. *Anytime*."

"Damn, I really gotta go now. You gon' get me in trouble. Bye, Ms. Bobbie. Don't worry, if I even think about taking a drink, I'ma call you." He climbed into the car and waved at me before pulling out of the driveway.

I walked back inside and headed up to the nursery where Reggie was sitting in a rocking chair holding Faith in his arms. His eyes were closed and his face was a reflection of peace. I stood there and stared at the two of them for a long while. They were the pieces of my heart that allowed it to beat. They were my life's blood and my lifeline, and no one in the entire world could possibly understand what it meant to me to have my family back together, to know that despite my flaws and craziness, I had a man and a child who loved me anyway—unconditionally. And despite what had transpired between Reggie and Caprice, I loved him unconditionally, too. We could work through that. We could work through anything.

I thought about what the weeks ahead held for us. I wanted and needed to perform again, but first things first. I would need to get back into attending my AA meetings. I decided I'd call my sponsor in the morning. That only left one thing. I needed to talk to my mother and the girls.

I quietly left Reggie and Faith in the nursery and headed down the stairs where the scene in the living room was enough to break a gladiator's heart. Tomeka was in tears, curled up on the sofa next to Mama. Sharee was crying, too. Mama was rubbing Tomeka's arm and shaking her head.

"Can I come in?" I asked, not wanting to interrupt a private moment between the three of them.

"Of course you can. It's yo' house. And I thank Meka understands now."

I nodded and sat down across from them. "I'm sorry, Tomeka. I really am. I wish things could be different for you."

She snuffled and sniffled and curled up into a tighter ball.

"Mama, I was wondering if I could talk to you about something—you and the girls."

"Okay," Mama said. Sharee nodded. More sniffles from Tomeka.

"Um…the situation with Faith and everyone thinking I had something to do with it really took a toll on me. And, well…I started back to drinking." I felt my eyes well up with tears. "I…um, I need help. I'm gonna start back to attending my meetings every week and I just…I was wondering if you guys would stay here for a while longer and help us with Faith until I get myself back together. I wouldn't ask you, but…"

"Well, I had done already decided we was staying a while longer anyhow. I ain't letting no other stranger keep my grandbaby. I'll keep her. Shoot, I was thankin' y'all might could fix up dat little house out back for me and da' girls, and maybe we could jus' stay here."

"You mean move here, Granny?" Sharee asked.

Mama nodded. "If dat's alright wit' y'all two. I know you got friends back home, but I was thankin'; maybe it's time to move on. Only family I got leff' back home is my sister, Werdine, and half da' time we can't stand each other. Bobbie Ann and Reggie is our family and they need us and we need them."

"I think it'll be great, Granny," Sharee said with a smile.

Mama peered down at Tomeka. "How 'bout you, Meka. Whatchu thank?"

Tomeka sat up and wiped her puffy eyes and tear-streaked face. "I don't care. It doesn't matter where we live," she said solemnly.

Mama sighed. "Well, that settles it. We'll move out back, if it suits you and Reggie."

I smiled and felt a huge weight lift from my shoulders. "Thank you. Thank you, Mama. You don't have to move out back. You all can stay right here with us. Me and Reggie already talked about it on the ride here from Dallas."

Mama shook her head. "No, ma'am. You needs yo' privacy. Dat little house out back will suit us jus' fine."

"Okay. It was originally a guest cottage, but we're using it as a pool house. It's got two bedrooms and a nice little kitchen in it. We'll fix it up real nice for y'all. Thank you, again, Mama. Thanks, girls."

Tomeka's answer was to stand from the couch and slowly walk out of the room. She looked so sad. I really prayed that she'd be able to get over her heartache.

Forty-Two

"Walkin' And Cryin'"

Tomeka

My feet felt like they were made of lead as I walked through the house, up the stairs, and to my bedroom. I felt hopeless and lost. I climbed in the bed and tried to remember the words Abraham said to me on the way back to the house.

"No matter what happens or what I say, I want you to know that I love you, and we will be together. Just trust me, angel. We will be together."

I was trying to believe his words, but I just couldn't see how we would ever be together again. At that point, we couldn't even write to each other, and Granny had taken my phone from me. I would never see him again. I would never hear his voice again. I would never kiss him again. I had lost him. He wasn't going to wait until I was eighteen. It was over for us. But I loved him and my heart ached and the only thing I wanted to do was to die. But I was too scared of going to hell to kill myself.

I sat up in the bed and dug through my purse for the picture he'd sent to me a few months earlier. I kept it tucked behind another picture so Detective Sharee couldn't find it. As I dug through my purse, I noticed a piece of blue paper. *Where did that come from?* I pulled it out of my purse and unfolded it. The logo from the hotel Abraham and I were in was at the top of the page. As soon as I recognized the handwriting, I jumped up from the bed and locked the door. Then I sat down on the floor and began to read.

Dear Tomeka,

As I write this letter, we are together in the hotel. You're asleep right now, and you look just like an angel. Today has been the best day of my life. Being with you, kissing you, and touching you has all been a dream come true. I know you are young and maybe people won't approve of us being together, but I don't care. I love you, Tomeka. I love you with all of my heart and soul. I dream about you at night. I think about you every moment I am awake. I don't think I can stand to be apart from you anymore, not after today. Not after I know what it feels like to be with you and to touch you.

I'm going to try to do this the right way. I'm going to meet your family and ask for permission to keep you in my life. I'm pretty sure that with my record and my age, your family is going to say no. If they forbid us from being together, I want you to do something for me.

In three weeks, I want you to meet me at the park in your aunt's neighborhood. I'll figure out a way to get in the gate and past the guards. Don't worry about that. Meet me at midnight. Be careful, though, because if anything happened to you, I would die. I know three weeks is a long time to be apart, but I need that time to make arrangements for us to be together, and maybe your family will have calmed down a little by then and cut you some slack. Don't bring a suitcase or anything like that. I got a bunch of money saved up from before I got locked up, so I can buy you anything you need.

Tomeka, if you decide to leave with me, we'll have to go away from here, and you won't be able to see your family for a long time. If you leave Houston before then, please find a way to call me or write so that I can make other plans to meet you. If you don't show up or I don't hear from you, I'll understand. Either way, I love you, and I always will.

I wanted to ask you something when we were together today, but I lost my nerve. Tomeka, will you marry me? Because that's what I want more than anything in the world. I don't want you to be my girlfriend. I want you to be my wife. If you decide to meet me, to go away with me, I will know that you want the same thing.

I hope to see you in three weeks. I love you, my angel.

Love,

Abraham

I had a decision to make—a hard decision. But actually, I'd already made it. As much as I loved Abraham, I didn't want to worry Granny any more than I already had. I didn't want to cause trouble for my family. I just didn't want to hurt them. I closed my eyes and kissed the piece of paper then tucked it in my purse, unlocked the bedroom door, and went to bed.

Forty-Three

"Midnight Dreams"

Bobbie

I'm not sure what woke me up that night. I hadn't been sleeping well since we brought Faith back home, so any little noise was liable to wake me up anyway. But this time, it wasn't a noise; it was more of a feeling that something was wrong. Something just felt off.

I rolled over and looked at Reggie, who was sleeping like a baby. I climbed out of bed and walked across the room to Faith's crib. I breathed a sigh of relief when I saw her snuggled underneath her pink blanket, sleeping peacefully. I turned and looked around the dark bedroom, confused about what I was feeling. What was going on with me? Was I being paranoid? Was I losing my mind?

I walked back over to the bed and sat down on the edge, trying to understand the feeling that was still stirring inside of me, wondering what it meant.

I felt Reggie's hand on my back. "You okay, baby? What's wrong?" he asked groggily.

"I don't know," I said softly.

Reggie sat up and turned a lamp on. "What is it?"

"I…I don't know. Something just feels wrong. I just feel like something is going to happen."

"Like what?"

I looked at him, my heart racing. "I don't know, but I think it's happening right now."

Reggie stood from the bed and pulled on his pajama bottoms and a t-shirt.

"Where are you going?" I asked.

"To check the house. Stay here with Faith.

I nodded and walked back over to the crib and stood guard. I closed my eyes as I nervously tapped my foot and silently prayed. They still hadn't caught Francine or Vera or whoever she was. Was she back? Had she somehow gotten into the house again? Or was it Caprice? Had she managed to break out of jail?

Please, Lord, protect my baby. Please, please, please, Lord…

When Reggie finally returned to our bedroom, Mama and Sharee were with him. Mama looked like she would fall at any second.

"What…what is it? Where is Tomeka?" I asked.

Reggie handed me a letter and as I read it, my heart fell.

Dear Everyone,

I am so sorry things had to be this way. I had to make a choice, and it was hard. I had to choose between my family and my heart. I chose my heart. I am going to be with Abraham because I love him. I know none of you believe me, but I really do and he loves me, too. We are going away together.

Please don't try to find me. And please don't worry about me. I love you all, even you, Sharee. I wish I could've stayed. I tried to stay. I really did, but I just couldn't stand to be away from him anymore.

Love,

Tomeka

Epilogue

Tomeka

I rolled over in the bed and smiled at the sight of Abraham sleeping. We were somewhere in Mexico. Some small town that I couldn't pronounce the name of. But it didn't matter where we were as long as we were together. I reached over and softly brushed my hand over his hair. Then I leaned in and kissed his cheek.

He smiled and said, "Can't sleep?"

"No," I said. "I'm too excited."

He opened his eyes and looked into mine. "Well, you got plenty of time to sleep. We're going to be together forever."

"You promise?"

He nodded as he reached up and touched my lips with his finger. "Only death can take me away from you."

I smiled. "I love you so much."

"I love you, too. Lay back down, angel."

After I lay down next to him, Abraham reached for me and pulled me close to him. He kissed me and held me tightly, and all I could think about was how lucky I was to be with him. I rolled over, and he snuggled closely behind me.

Through the window across the room I could see the night sky. I could see a few small stars, and I thought about Arkansas and my old home and my sister and my grandmother. I thought about how badly I used to want to leave there and go away. I was away now. Far away. And I was happy. After sneaking away from my aunt's house, we'd driven all that night and most of the next day until we reached the border.

Now we were free. No one could tell us what to do. No school or rules for me. I was a woman, an adult, and no one could tell me who to be with. Abraham and I loved each other, and we belonged together. Now nothing and no one could keep us apart.

For more information on alcohol addiction and recovery, visit:

http://www.aa.org

To learn how you can help find the missing, visit:

http://www.missingkids.com/

To learn more about the author, visit:

http://adriennethompsonwrites.webs.com/

Follow Adrienne on Twitter!

https://twitter.com/A_H_Thompson

Like Adrienne on Facebook!

https://www.facebook.com/pages/Author-Adrienne-Thompson/300208429995218

Follow Adrienne on Pinterest!

http://pinterest.com/ahthompsn/boards/

Excerpt from Your Love Is King

(Coming Soon)

I rolled over in the bed after a short nap, opened my eyes, and nearly jumped out of my skin. For a brief moment, I'd forgotten that Darius was lying in bed with me. The sight of him lying there asleep with his mouth wide open startled me. I eyed him with disgust as I tried to ease out of bed undetected. I slid and slid until my feet finally reached the floor, tipped through the cluttered efficiency apartment into the bathroom, and peered into the smudged mirror. *What are you doing, Marli Meadows?* I wondered. *Why are you here with him?* I shook my head as if the mere action could erase my relationship with Darius Cotton right out of my life.

I squatted over the toilet and relieved myself—afraid to sit on the seat. Knowing Darius, there was no telling how many other butts had been on that seat. I turned the water in the faucet on to a slow trickle, still not wanting to awaken Darius, and washed my hands. I dried them with some toilet paper and then quickly pulled my underwear and work uniform back on and slowly opened the creaky bathroom door.

I exited the bathroom and found Darius sitting on the side of the bed, lighting up a blunt. *Dang!* I thought, *if I don't get out of here quick, I'll be smelling just like that stuff and probably get a contact high. It'd be my luck for them to pop up with a random drug test at work and that crap'll show up.*

"You leaving, baby?" he grunted between drags. He rubbed his hand across his bare chest and stretched. I eyed his nakedness as I walked back into the room.

"Yeah, it's already eleven. I gotta go home and get some rest for work tonight," I answered as I gathered up my purse and slipped on my shoes.

With a lopsided grin on his face, he revealed two rows of shiny gold teeth and said, "Yeah, 'cause you know if you stay here you gone have to put in some more work, huh?"

Ugh, I thought. "Yeah, well I'll talk to you later, Darius."

"A'ight, come give me a kiss, boo."

I swallowed hard. I know this sounds strange considering the fact that I'd just had sex with him, but the thought of kissing him really didn't appeal to me. It took all I had in me to walk over to him, bend over, and plant a kiss on his dark lips.

He swatted my butt. "A'ight girl, I'll holla at you later. Don't work too hard, tonight."

I nodded. "I won't. Bye, Darius."

"Bye, Mar-lay."

I shook my head as I closed the door behind me. We'd been "seeing" each other for nearly two years and he still mispronounced my name. Well, it was either that or he was just so country that it *sounded* like he was mispronouncing it. Whichever was the case, it was irritating.

I walked down the steep stairs from Darius's apartment out onto the parking lot. I unlocked and then climbed into my Toyota Camry which was parked right next to Darius's souped-up Chevy Caprice. I rolled my eyes at the repeated Louis Vuitton logos covering his car. I backed out of my space and glanced at his license plate which read, SMOKONE, and sighed as I pulled off the lot.

Excerpt From Ain't Nobody

(Coming Soon)

Prologue

Sometimes a woman's just had enough, no matter how she may feel about a man. No matter how much she loves him and wants to be with him, there's always that one teeny tiny little straw—the *last* straw. It usually pops up after she's done all she can humanly possibly do to make things work. She's cooked for him, cleaned for him, praised him, had sex with him, ignored his annoying ways, and yet she still finds herself holding the short end of the stick.

As I sat there on the side of Quincy's bed, the last straw flew in threw the bedroom window and landed right on my camel's back. Quincy, my fiancé and the love of my life, was in the shower whistling. He was whistling like he didn't have a care in the world. He was whistling like I wasn't thirty-seven and kicking the hell out of forty. He was whistling like I wasn't unmarried and childless. Like we hadn't been engaged for five years. *Five years.* He was whistling like he hadn't refused to set a wedding date. Like my biological clock wasn't ticking as loud as a time bomb.

I'd been with Quincy Wright for eight years. I'd been his lover and friend. I'd bent over backwards, neglected my own needs, and done all I could do to be a good woman. I wanted a husband and I wanted children and he knew it. We'd discussed it at length. And what was his response?

His black behind was in the shower whistling. That was it and whether he knew it or not, it was over. O-V-E-R.

www.ingramcontent.com/pod-product-compliance
Lightning Source LLC
Chambersburg PA
CBHW070007260626
47159CB00005B/1706